W9-DFC-162

Shadow
AND THE GUNNER

By the same author

ME, CHOLAY & CO—APACHE WARRIORS
KIDNAPPING MR. TUBBS
MAYBE NEXT SUMMER

Shadow
AND THE GUNNER
by Don Schellie

FOUR WINDS PRESS NEW YORK

LIBRARY OF CONGRESS CATALOGING IN
PUBLICATION DATA

Schellie, Don, 1932–
    Shadow and the Gunner.

    Summary: A young boy growing up in Chicago during
World War II recalls his friendship with his idol, the older
boy next door.
    [1. Friendship—Fiction. 2. World War, 1939–1945—
Fiction] I. Title.
PZ7.S3433Sh 1982   [Fic]   82–70415
ISBN 0–590–07643–4   AACR2

PUBLISHED BY FOUR WINDS PRESS

A DIVISION OF SCHOLASTIC INC., NEW YORK, N.Y.

COPYRIGHT © 1982 BY DON SCHELLIE

ALL RIGHTS RESERVED

PRINTED IN THE UNITED STATES OF AMERICA

LIBRARY OF CONGRESS CATALOG CARD NUMBER: 82–70415

1 2 3 4 5 86 85 84 83 82

For my brother Jim, who was there.
And for Marie and Kari.
And in memory of Jamie.

ALL MY TEACHERS CALL ME ROBERT, AND MOM and Dad call me that, too, when I've done something I shouldn't have. Otherwise, Mom calls me Bobby, and so does my snotty sister, Shirley, and most of my other relatives except for Dad and my big brother, Russ. They usually call me Bob, and that suits me fine. The guys at school call me Simpson, which is my last name, or they shorten it to Simp, and that's okay, too. You can call me Bob, if you want to, or Simp or Simpson or even Bobby, but please don't call me Shadow.

Gunner's the only one who ever called me that, so it's a special name between the two of us, like Gunner was my special name for him. He was really Billy Eckert, but I called him Gunner because right after he graduated from high school he went into the air corps and got to be a tail gunner on a B-24 Liberator that helped bomb the Nazis off the map.

Don't ask me where he got that name for me, because I sure don't know. A long time ago, when I was just a little kid, he started calling me Shadow, and that was it. Whenever I'd ask him why he called me that, he'd grin and tell me to guess.

Once I guessed he called me that because "The Shadow" is one of my favorite radio programs. It comes on at four-thirty every Sunday afternoon, and I always listen to it. Another time I asked if he got the name from that funny little guy named Shadow in the "Harold Teen" comic strip in the Chicago *Tribune* funnies.

Gunner never told me for sure. I think he just wanted me to keep guessing forever.

And now I'll never know, not that it matters a whole lot. Except Gunner was the only person who ever called me Shadow and it made me feel swell when he did, because he was real special. But now Gunner is gone.

Chapter One

I COULDN'T HELP THAT I HATED SHIRLEY
more than I ever hated anybody in the world. Even more
than Adolf Hitler himself. Or Hirohito, the emperor of
Japan. At least I didn't have to do dishes with Emperor
Hirohito every night after supper, or pretend that I just
loved Hitler, the way I had to do with Shirley whenever
our parents were around. She's my sister.

The trouble was, she had to go and butt in and ruin
everything between Gunner and me. You can understand
why I hated her so much.

★ 3 ★

Right away I should have realized what was happening because I had turned eleven and figured I knew plenty about girls and love and everything else. Only I couldn't imagine Gunner falling in love with anybody, especially with Shirley. But that's exactly what happened that October, right before my very own eyes, and there wasn't a thing I could do about it.

Or maybe I just didn't want to believe it, because I was so excited about his being home on leave and our doing things together the way we used to. For days before Gunner got home, I was excited about it, and by that Friday I was jumpy as nine thousand grasshoppers.

Friday afternoons in school are always the longest, anyway, but that Friday it seemed three o'clock would never come. I'll bet I looked at the clock a thousand times, but the hands hardly moved at all.

It was lucky we were having silent reading. If we'd been doing geography or arithmetic or something where you have to pay attention because maybe you'll be called on next to recite or go to the blackboard, I'd have been in trouble.

But Miss Connelly was at her desk pretending to read. Everybody knew she was really sleeping, though, thinking nobody could see that her eyes were closed behind her glasses.

My seat is way in the back of the room, right behind Laverne, so I didn't even bother holding my book up like I was really reading it, because Miss Connelly can't see me from her desk, even when she's awake. That's the good thing about Laverne. She's big.

I was disgusted and I stretched and made a loud sigh

that came out a squeal and everybody heard it, and somebody up in front laughed. It was Juicy. We call him that because his teeth are sort of wide apart, so when he talks he spatters spit all over you. When you talk to Juicy, you have to stand way back. Except for that he's okay, and he's my second-best friend, next to Gunner.

For a long time I stared through the big windows on the other side of the room, wishing I was outside, running home. Then, for maybe the hundredth time since recess, I read everything that was written on the front blackboard. I almost had it memorized. Up in the right-hand corner teacher had written, "Miss Connelly, Room 303, 6th Grade." Below it was the date—"Friday, Sept. 29, 1944."

In the middle of the board it said the girls had bought $11.25 worth of war stamps that day, and that the boys had bought $7.75 worth. Every Friday is war stamp day and usually the girls beat us. I don't know where they get all their money. We beat them in the scrap-paper drive, though, and that makes up for it. There was a reminder on the board that Tuesday was scrap-paper day, as if we needed a reminder. Every Tuesday is scrap-paper day and we have to bring in all the old newspapers and magazines and cardboard boxes we can collect in the neighborhood. We're always collecting something for the war effort. If it isn't scrap paper, then we're collecting old tires or tin cans or scrap metal. It isn't easy being patriotic. Winning a war takes a lot of hard work.

The Japs attacked Pearl Harbor on December 7, 1941, but it seems as though the war has been going on lots longer than three years. Sometimes I can hardly even remember what it was like before the war. It's just about the only thing anybody ever talks about.

For a while after Pearl Harbor everybody was afraid the Japs or Nazis were going to bomb Chicago, so at night we couldn't let any lights show from our houses. They call that a blackout. At school we had air-raid drills. We still do. But after a while we started winning the war so we don't worry so much anymore about being bombed. I looked up at the clock again and it was still only twenty to three. I crossed my arms on my desk and put my head down on them.

I thought about how nice it would be if we had a fire drill, or even an air-raid drill. They always make time go faster. I like fire drills best. When we have a fire drill we go outside into the school yard and wait for the school to burn down. It never does. When we have an air-raid drill all we do is line up in threes and march down to the first floor and huddle along the walls, hoping a bomb won't fall on us. So that afternoon there wasn't a fire drill and there wasn't even an air-raid drill. There never is when you really need one.

Nothing I did seemed to make the time go any faster, and all I could think about was that Gunner was coming home!

On Wednesday he had telephoned his folks long distance from New Jersey, and said he was back in the United States and that he'd be home on furlough Friday and could stay for a month.

I could hardly wait, because I hadn't seen Gunner since February, when he was home for two weeks before he went overseas. Ever since then he had been in England, flying bombing missions over Germany. He'd have some swell stories to tell about what it was like being in the war, and I knew I'd have a lot of fun being with him while he was home. It was always fun being with Gunner.

I wondered if he would look any different. I decided that he wouldn't. Gunner wouldn't have changed at all. With my eyes shut I tried to remember exactly what he looked like. His hair was brown and before he went into the air corps and got a crew cut it was wavy, and his eyes were the color of the sky on a clear spring day. The girls all said he was handsome.

As far back as I can remember, I've known Gunner. He and my brother Russ were best friends, even before they started kindergarten together. Our families have lived next door to each other for a long time.

Mom works afternoons and Saturdays in that insurance office up on Belmont Avenue, so when I was smaller, Russ had to keep an eye on me after school and all day Saturday. Russ hated having to take care of me.

I liked it, though. It was lots more fun being with the big guys, like Russ and Billy and their friends, than with the kids my own age, even though I have good pals of my own, like Juicy and Ralph.

Billy was amazing. Maybe someday they'll make a Billy Eckert comic book about him. Like once, a long time before the Japs attacked Pearl Harbor, Billy hopped all the way to school on one foot. And that's four blocks! I wasn't there, but Russ told me all about it. He said Billy had hopped around the school yard until the bell rang.

When his class lined up at the door, he kept standing on that one foot, and then he hopped inside and up the stairs to the third floor. He was into the classroom and almost to his desk when Miss Byrnes made him quit hopping. She scolded him for disrupting the class, even though the tardy bell hadn't even rung. She is still as crabby as that.

All the kids liked Billy, but so did the old people. Once I was sitting on the curb in front of the Wendts' house watching the big guys play softball, when the old Tomaszek sisters came along carrying shopping bags of groceries. They are old maids and they live with their mother who is at least ninety or maybe even a hundred. The sisters must be in their seventies, Mom says. Anyway, even though Billy was at bat, he called time out so he could carry the sisters' groceries all the way to their house, way at the other end of the block. They tried to give him a nickel for helping, but he wouldn't even take it.

After my brother Russ quit high school and enlisted in the army, Billy sort of looked out for me, even though nobody asked him to. That's when we got to be such extra good friends.

With my head down on the desk and my eyes closed, I guess I must've fallen asleep. Next thing I knew the warning bell was ringing at five minutes to three.

I was ready to leave in a second, and everybody else was, except teacher. While we waited, she gathered up all the papers she had to take home to grade over the weekend. Finally she was ready.

She walked to the door and turned out the lights, then told us we could line up. It was like a big explosion with everybody running to the door at once. Usually when we're that noisy she makes us go back to our seats and wait until the three o'clock bell, and then line up quietly, but she must've been eager to get home, too, that Friday, because she didn't say one word to us. She scowled, though. Miss Connelly's always scowling.

We lined up in threes along the side blackboard. While we waited for the bell there was a lot of whispering, and Kenny Gretz reached up and untied the bow on the back of Eleanor's dress and she turned around and slugged him in the eye and everybody laughed except Kenny. Teacher pretended she didn't see it. At last the three o'clock bell rang and we marched out of the room, along the hallway, and down the stairs.

When we hit the outside door, I started running right away. I didn't wait for Juicy and Ed and Ralph at the school-yard gate, the way I always do. We walk home together all the time, but we mess around and it takes us about a half hour, but that Friday I was in a hurry.

It's four long blocks from school to my house, and I ran almost the whole way without stopping.

Chapter Two

I WOULDN'T HAVE HAD TO RUN BECAUSE BILLY
wasn't even home yet. I knew he wasn't because Mrs.
Eckert was watching through the lace curtains in the
front window, right next to Billy's service flag. A service
flag has a blue star on a white field, with a wide red
border around it. When you see one in a window you
know somebody who lives there is in the army or navy or
something.

Anyway, Mrs. Eckert sure wouldn't have been watching like that if Billy had been there. So I waved to her as

I passed and went on home. Nobody was there, so I decided to rake the leaves while I waited for Billy. Otherwise, Dad would be after me to do them over the weekend.

I started raking slowly, keeping an eye out for Billy. Mr. Eckert was at work—he works in a defense plant that makes radios for tanks—so Billy's Uncle George was going to meet him down at the LaSalle Street train depot. As I raked I watched for Billy's uncle's car, and about all I could think of was that I'd be seeing Billy before long. I was excited about that—almost as excited as Billy himself had been on the day he enlisted. The day after he graduated from high school in June 1943, he got up early and rode an Addison Street bus downtown and enlisted in the army air corps. Billy loved airplanes, and more than anything else, he wanted to fly in the war.

A bunch of us had been playing softball in the street that afternoon when Billy came around the corner, cut across the Orlowskis' front lawn, and headed for his house. On his face was the biggest grin I'd ever seen. The second I saw that smile I knew he had passed his tests. Billy wasn't very tall, but just then he walked like he was about fifteen feet tall. I hollered for time out and ran to meet him.

"Shake hands with Buck Private William H. Eckert," he called, putting his hand out, "of the United States Army Air Corps!" I pumped his hand like I was turning a long jump rope for the girls, then stepped back and saluted him. He snapped to attention and returned the salute and pretended to poke his thumb in his eye and acted real silly about it, like in an Abbott and Costello

★ 11 ★

picture. Juicy and Ralph and Ed came over then, and Juicy, bobbing his red head back and forth, started singing, "You're in the army now, you're not behind a plow, you'll never get rich, you son of a—" And before he could say the word, Billy reached out and clamped his hand over Juicy's mouth and wrestled him to the ground. Juicy shouted that he "gave" and Billy let him up. We all walked with Billy to his house, and he told us what he'd done downtown. There were all kinds of dumb tests he had taken, he said, and lots of forms he had to fill out.

"And then came the physical!" said Billy, laughing. "You never saw anything funnier in all your life. There were maybe a hundred guys in that big room, and nobody had on a stitch of clothes except for the doctor and the medic who was helping him." Billy paused for a minute and laughed again. "Anyway, we all tried to act casual—like we were used to being in rooms full of naked guys, but everybody was real embarrassed. You just couldn't help it!"

Then Billy shooed us off to finish the game because he had to go inside and tell his folks his good news. I didn't feel much like playing anymore, but I did. I struck out my next time up, so I quit and went inside to listen to my programs on the radio.

He had five days at home before he was to report for duty, and the time went by awfully fast. The night before he left, Billy came over to say good-bye to our family, I remembered as I raked the leaves.

Mom and Shirley and Dad and I sat around the kitchen table with Billy, who was in Russ's chair. Mom wanted to make some lemonade or coffee or get out the cookie jar, but he said he couldn't eat or even drink a thing because his mom had been stuffing him with all his favorite things. Anyway, he couldn't stay but a minute.

"Frank McGowan says he's sorry you're leaving so quickly," my father said. "He'd hoped to have a farewell block party for you." Mr. McGowan is our block captain and is in charge of our war effort. He tries to have a block party for all our boys as they go into the service, like the one for Russ.

"Do you know yet where you'll be stationed?" asked Shirley.

Billy shook his head. "Tomorrow we're going to Fort Sheridan, but we'll just be there a few days for processing. After that—who knows? I'll send Ma my address soon as I have one."

Billy looked at his watch—it was the new military one that his family had given him for graduation—and said he had to be running along.

Mom gave Billy a hug and as she kissed him, she started to cry. He held her close and patted her back. "You're like another son to us, Billy. God take care of you."

Billy smiled and Dad took his hand and held it for a minute in both of his. "Take care, son," Dad said then, "and give 'em hell for me, will you, Billy? I just wish I was a few years younger so I could—"

"Now, Carl, don't you start talking like that again," said Mom. "Let the boy be on his way."

"You already had your war, Mr. Simpson," Billy told Dad, and then he slipped his arm around Dad's shoulder and squeezed. Dad shrugged and laughed uneasily. He had been what they called a doughboy in the army in World War I, and was aboard a troopship headed for France on November 11, 1918, the day the Germans surrendered, so he hadn't seen any action. He felt hurt and hardly ever talked about how he missed out on the big war.

Billy turned to Shirley then.

"We'll miss you, Bill," she told him. "All of us will." As he moved closer to her, Shirley put her hand out for him to shake.

"That the best you can do?" he asked, pushing aside her hand. "Least a guy marching off to war can expect is a kiss from the little girl next door." He leaned forward and kissed her right on the mouth.

"*Bil*-ly!" she said, and for a second she looked mad, but then her face softened and she laughed with the rest of us.

"C'mon, Shadow," he said. "Got something for you over at the house." As we cut across the grass, Billy laid his arm on my shoulder.

At the front steps of his house, we stopped. "It's not going to seem the same with you gone, Billy," I managed to say. "I'll miss you."

"Bet you won't at all. You'll have plenty to keep you busy. And just you wait—this war'll be over and I'll be home before you know it."

We went inside and Mr. and Mrs. Eckert were in the living room, listening to "Fibber McGee and Molly" on the radio. As usual, Mrs. Eckert was crocheting. Just as we walked in, Fibber opened his closet door and all the junk fell out and crashed to the floor, and we couldn't help but laugh. It happens every week on that program, and it's still funny, no matter how many times you hear it.

Billy's parents are older than mine. In fact, Mrs. Eckert looks like somebody's grandmother, but she isn't. Her hair is gray, with tight little curls around her face. She wears glasses and is sort of fat. She's a good cook and before the war she used to bake lots of cookies and cakes and bring them over to us. Since the war started and sugar and butter have been rationed, she doesn't bake as much.

"What do you hear from that brother of yours?" she asked.

"Not much," I said. "We had a short letter from him Monday, but no news. Russ says he's still fighting the battle of Texas, and he'd really like to get overseas, but they just keep him there typewriting letters and reports. He hates it."

"Our Billy should be so lucky," said Mrs. Eckert, sighing, and the mister frowned and said, "Now, Naomi, don't you talk like that," and he reached out and patted her hand. Her eyes were red and I could see she'd been crying. I guess even Fibber McGee and Molly couldn't cheer her up that night.

I followed Billy into his bedroom and he went to his closet and brought out his cigar boxes of marbles and lagging cards. I counted seven boxes.

"For months I've been meaning to give you these, Shadow," he said, handing me the stack of boxes. "You can put them to lots better use than I can. Don't guess they play marbles much in the air corps."

"Aw, Billy," I said, "you should keep 'em. Maybe after the war you'll want to lag cards."

He laughed. "That's a long time off, Shadow, and no telling how things will be then. Besides, if I remember right, about half of these cards and marbles I won off your brother. Russ never was much good at lagging cards or shooting marbles."

"Okay, if you're sure. . . ."

"Sure, I'm sure, pal," he said. "Besides, Ma'll be tickled pink to have 'em out of my closet." The boxes weren't heavy, but they were awkward to carry. I said good night to the Eckerts and went outside and down the front steps to the sidewalk, balancing the boxes carefully as I could. Billy stood in the open doorway.

"So long, Shadow," he called after me. "You take care of the neighborhood. You're one of the big guys now."

I stood up straight, tall as I could, then stopped and turned. " 'Bye, Billy," I called, keeping the tears back, and as I turned, my ankle twisted in the soft grass and the pile of cigar boxes jiggled for an instant and then went flying out of my arms.

Every last one of them! Bubblegum cards and marbles —there must have been ten thousand marbles alone— went flying in every direction, and I took a nosedive!

Laughing, Billy bounced down the steps and in two seconds was kneeling beside me.

"Hurt, Shadow?" he asked, touching my shoulder.

"Naw," I said, "My knees sting, but I'm not hurt. Not really."

"Good," he said. "Way you went flying, I was afraid maybe you'd broken your neck. Now, let's get these things picked up." With both hands he started scooping up marbles and dropping them into the boxes.

"Never mind, Billy. You don't have to do that. I can pick 'em up. It was my own fault."

"Forget it. Two of us—we'll have the job done in a couple of minutes."

So Buck Private Billy Eckert and I sat on the grass picking up bubblegum cards and all those thousands of marbles. Neither of us said anything for a while, but soon Billy started laughing again, only harder than before.

"What's so funny?" I asked him.

"This," he said. "This is funny. Bet I'm the only guy in the whole United States of America who spent his last night home before he went off to war playing with marbles and lagging cards!" He dropped another handful of marbles into a box and shut the lid.

That started me laughing, too. I guess it *was* funny, when you thought of it that way. So Billy laughed and the more he laughed, the harder I laughed, but then I realized I wasn't just laughing, but partly crying, too, only I tried not to let Billy know.

Just remembering that as I raked, I laughed again, and then I heard a car horn honking. I looked around just as a big, old black Hudson pulled off Central Avenue, onto our street, its horn tooting all the way. I recognized the car. It was Billy's uncle's.

Gunner was home!

Chapter Three

BILLY WAS HOME ALMOST ALL OF OCTOBER, but in some ways it hardly seemed that long. In other ways it seemed longer. At first he acted the way he always had, and I think everything would have been okay if it hadn't been for Shirley. All of a sudden he just seemed to discover her, like when you find a wart you didn't know you had and you just can't leave it alone.

That Friday afternoon as the Hudson pulled up in front of the Eckerts' house, I dropped the rake and ran to the curb, scattering the pile of leaves every which way.

Billy's mother must've still been watching through the curtains, because she came through the front door faster than I'd ever seen her move and hurried down the front sidewalk, her arms outstretched. "Billy, Billy, Billy," she called.

Gunner jumped from the car and ran to meet her and they hugged and kissed and cried and then stepped apart to look at each other, then hugged and kissed and cried some more. Billy's Uncle George got out of the car and opened a rear door and pulled Billy's luggage from the back seat. There was a big canvas duffel bag and a cloth suitcase that Billy called his B-4 bag.

I stood back while Billy and his mother did all that hugging and kissing, and then he spied me. "Shadow, you little son of a gun," he hollered, and he turned to me like he was going to hug me, too. I stuck out my hand to shake. "Hi, Gunner—welcome home!" That was a silly thing to say, I know, but I couldn't think of anything better. We shook hands and he put an arm around my shoulder.

Billy's uncle gave Mrs. Eckert a kiss on the cheek. "Got to get to work, Naomi," he said. "Tell Harold hello."

"You can't stay for a cup of coffee, George?" she asked. "I baked a cake."

"You know I'd like to, but duty calls." He shook hands with Billy and then drove off. I don't know what Billy's uncle does for a living, but it must be important. He has a "C" gasoline rationing sticker on his car's windshield, which means he can get about all the gasoline he needs.

My dad only has a "B" card, and he always wishes he had more gas, even though he's lots better off than someone who has an "A" sticker. They hardly get any gasoline at all.

Billy looked swell in his uniform. He wore his hat cocked over to one side, the way Smilin' Jack does in the *Tribune* comics. His woolen uniform was that brownish green color called olive drab. On the lapels of the coat were the shiny brass insignia of the air corps, with the spread wings and the propeller in the middle.

Over the top left pocket of his uniform jacket were five colored ribbons, three on the lower row and two above it. The ribbons stood for medals he had been given, and I hoped he'd tell me about them. Above the ribbons were his silver aerial gunner's wings, and sewn to his left shoulder was a round insignia with a big gold "8" in it. That meant Billy was in the Eighth Air Force. On his sleeves were staff sergeant's stripes.

"C'mon, Shadow," he said, "give me a hand with these bags." He took off his uniform hat and put it on my head and it went way down, over my ears. Billy picked up his duffel bag like it didn't weigh anything, and slung it up on one shoulder. He put his other arm around his mom and they started toward the house. I carried the B-4 bag.

Inside the living room, Billy told me to put the bag anyplace, and he'd take it to the bedroom later.

"By the way, I've got something for you," Billy told me. "After I get unpacked I'll bring it over. Probably after supper."

"You didn't have to bring me anything, Gunner," I

said, but I was glad he did. I wondered what it could be.

"But, right now, Ma and I have lots of talking to do—a lot of catching up."

"Yeah," I said, "and I've got my raking to finish." I wished Mrs. Eckert would offer me a piece of that cake she had mentioned, but she probably didn't think of it because she was so excited to see her son. I went outside and got back to work.

Before he went to England in February, Billy had been home a few times on furlough. One time he had just gotten his gunner's wings. He was proud about that and he was excited, too, because he had just found out he was going to be a tail gunner on a B-24 Liberator bomber, and that was his favorite ship. I asked him how he got to be a *tail* gunner instead of a waist gunner or something, and he reached out and messed up my hair.

"'Cause I'm such a little runt," he said. "Any guy who gets through gunnery school who can walk under a clothesline without knocking off his hat, they make a tail gunner." We both laughed.

It was while he was home that time that I started calling Billy "Gunner." I knew a lot of other Billys, I told him, but he was the only Gunner I knew. I think he liked having a special name.

Then he was gone again for three months. It seemed like I was always telling Billy good-bye. In February he came home for a fifteen-day furlough. Billy was terribly restless on that leave, and he was itching to get into action. It wasn't long before he got his wish. He and his crew got to England in March, and that's where he'd been until this time when he came home on furlough.

★ 21 ★

After supper I'd be hearing all about the bombing missions he'd flown over Germany, I thought as I raked. I could hardly wait, I was so excited.

Finally I had all the leaves in a pile beside the curb, and there wasn't any wind, so I started them burning. The flames spread quickly through the dry leaves, and in a couple of minutes the fire was going well.

I stood watching it and enjoying the smell, poking at the fire now and again with the rake, and when it was burned out, I swept the ashes together because it was about time for my programs. But then Shirley came around the corner, walking with Jeannine, who lives down the block near Linder Avenue. They almost looked as though they were in uniform, like WACs or WAVEs or lady marines.

Both were wearing plaid woolen skirts and pullover sweaters with blouse collars showing at the neck, and both had on white bobby socks and brown penny loafers. Both even carried an armful of school books. They were talking about something—boys, I suppose—but when they got close to me they shut up.

Sometimes I hear them talking about that skinny Frank Sinatra who wears bowties all the time and has the girls screaming and swooning about his singing. Sometimes I hear them talking about Dinah Shore or Jimmy or Tommy Dorsey, or about Glenn Miller, and they talk about them like they're real good friends from school or something. Especially Frank Sinatra and Glenn Miller.

They told each other good-bye and Shirley turned up our front walk and Jeannine kept right on walking toward her house. She didn't even say hello to me. She never does.

"Gunner's home," I said to Shirley.

"You mean *Bill?*" she asked. Of course she knew I meant *Bill*.

"Yeah," I said, following her along the sidewalk to our backyard. She opened the gate and let it swing shut behind her instead of holding it for me. I had to put down the rake to pull the gate open.

"I just know Mrs. Eckert was thrilled to see him," she said, sounding as though she really wasn't interested at all.

"They hugged and kissed out in front enough times to make up for all the months he was away," I said. "You could tell she was happy."

"Oh," said Shirley, sounding bored.

"What's for dinner?" I asked.

"Don't ask me. Mom didn't say. Macaroni and cheese, maybe." She went inside and I took the rake and basket back to the garage. Macaroni—nuts! We have that all the time and I hate it. But Mom says that with the shortages and with meat being rationed and so hard to get, even if you have ration stamps, we should be thankful even for macaroni and cheese. When I make a face about it, she scolds me and says to think of all those poor, starving children in China. I try to think about them, but it doesn't make the macaroni and cheese taste any better. I'll bet those Chinese kids would hate macaroni and cheese, too, if they had to have it for dinner as often as I do.

The bedroom I share with Russ is in the back of the

house, by the kitchen. Off our dining room is a little hallway that leads to Mom and Dad's bedroom, which is the front one, and to the middle bedroom, where Shirley sleeps. The bathroom is between those two bedrooms. After raking and burning the leaves, I wanted to wash my hands, but I knew Shirley would be in the bathroom already, so I washed at the kitchen sink.

I think Shirley spends half her life in the bathroom. I sometimes wonder what she finds to do in there that takes so much time. She had the radio in her bedroom turned on already, and she was listening to one of those disk jockeys who talk and play records. When she isn't listening to the radio she's playing Russ's phonograph, which she moved into her own bedroom when he went into the army. Or else she's going around the house singing songs and trying to sound just like the Modernaires or Dinah Shore or else all three Andrews Sisters at the same time.

Shirley loves music. Sometimes on Saturday afternoons she rides the Irving Park Road streetcar up to the record store on Milwaukee Avenue and goes into one of those little booths, and listens to records for hours. Once I went with her, but never again! She listened to records for two hours. Talk about a wasted afternoon! She usually buys one record every week and sometimes two. They cost thirty-five cents each and she must own a hundred-dollars worth of records. Someday I'd like to break every last one of them, I get so disgusted with her and her music. Dad always shakes his head when he finds out she bought a new one, and he asks her if she thinks thirty-five centses grow on trees. She just smiles and kisses Dad on his forehead, and he blushes and doesn't say anything more about it.

I went into my bedroom and shut the door and turned on my radio and tuned it to WENR. It was almost five o'clock and time for "Terry and the Pirates." After that, "Dick Tracy" comes on, and then, "Jack Armstrong," and then, "Captain Midnight." Of all the afternoon serials, I like "Captain Midnight" best. There's a bad guy on it named Ivan Shark, and you get all shivery just listening to him. Sometimes at the end of the program Captain Midnight gives out a message in secret code and you use your Captain Midnight decoder to find out what the message says.

Even with the door shut, Shirley's music almost drowned out "Terry and the Pirates." She had it loud enough for Jeannine to hear way down by Linder Avenue. You'd think she was deaf.

Shirley turned seventeen in August and Mom let her start wearing lipstick and other makeup. All of a sudden then, she was wanting to wear high-heeled shoes and silk stockings, like she was a grown-up lady.

For a sister she's pretty enough, I guess. Her hair is long and nearly blond, and she puts it up in curlers and a hairnet every night so people will think it's naturally curly. Well, it isn't, I know. Like most everybody in our family, she has blue eyes. Hers are bigger than everybody else's, though, and she doesn't let any of us forget that for a second. She can make her eyelids flutter like a butterfly. It's disgusting.

I wish you could see her at home. She takes a bath almost every night. Nobody can get that dirty, no matter how hard you try, unless you shovel coal for a living. She's the cleanest person I've ever known. When she isn't taking a bath, she's combing or brushing her hair and I bet she'll wear it out by the time she's twenty. Dad says it's just a stage Shirley's going through, but even he gets peeved when she locks herself in the bathroom for hours and nobody else can use the tub or sink or even the toilet.

For a while I sat at my desk, drawing pictures and listening to the radio, but then I got tired of drawing and stretched out on my bed. Russ and I have bunk beds and when he's home I sleep on the top deck. I like it better up there, except for the time I had a bad dream and rolled over the rail and fell to the floor. I didn't break anything, though.

When Russ is away, Mom makes me sleep on the lower bunk because it's easier to make up than the upper one. I lay there that afternoon, listening to the radio, with my toes stuck up into the springs of the upper bunk, and I kept thinking about what Billy and I were going to do while he was home on furlough. We'd sure have lots of fun together, that much I knew. And I wondered what he had brought me. I could hardly wait to find out.

I must've been really tired because I fell asleep halfway through "Jack Armstrong" and didn't hear Mom and Dad get home from work. Next thing I knew it was almost time for supper.

Chapter Four

DAD CAME INTO MY BEDROOM AND TURNED off the radio and the second he did that I woke up. I blinked and rubbed at the sleep in my eyes and it took me a minute to know what day it was and whether it was morning or what. Dad stood beside my bed with one hand on the upper bunk.

"How's the little guy?" he asked.

"Pretty good," I answered. "How's the big guy?"

"He's pretty good, too," he said. "Glad it's Friday, though. One more day to go."

My father is a carpenter and since the war started he's been working long shifts six days a week and sometimes seven, building war plants. At night when he comes home he's always real tired. He never says so, but I can tell by the look in his eyes and by the way he moves. He's tall and pretty skinny, but he's strong as anything, even though he doesn't look like a muscleman.

Everybody says I get my coloring from Dad. Both of us have blue eyes and light brown hair, but not as light as Shirley's. Dad's hair has some gray in it and it's always messed up because he wears a cap when he works and his head gets sweaty.

"Billy's home," I said, as I sat up and pulled on my gym shoes.

"So I hear," said Dad. "How's he look?"

"He looks swell."

Dad said it would be good to see Billy again. As I finished tying my shoes, he reached into the pocket of his overalls and I could hear coins jingle.

"Paper?" I asked, and he nodded and put three pennies into my hand. He said I didn't have to rush.

"Your mother went to the Red Cross after work and gave blood, so we're running a little behind." Every month Mom and Dad give a pint of blood to help the wounded soldiers and sailors. Dad says he can't afford to buy a lot of war bonds, but at least he can give blood. I dropped the newspaper pennies into my pocket and stood up.

Dad is a great one for keeping up with what is happening in the world, especially the war news. He listens to the news on the radio, and every evening he sends me over to Doc's drugstore to buy the late edition of the Chicago *Daily News*. On Sunday he reads the *Tribune*. So there isn't much Dad doesn't know about the war.

When I stepped into the kitchen, Mom was at the sink, peeling potatoes. I kissed her and said hi and then I sniffed. Something smelled awfully good, and it sure wasn't macaroni and cheese. I asked her what was for dinner.

"I splurged on ration points," Mom said. "I stopped at Heckman's butcher shop and got some ground round steak and made meatloaf. It'll have to do for two meals, though."

"Browned potatoes?" I asked. She smiled and nodded. She knows meatloaf and browned potatoes is one of my favorite meals.

"It's so hard to know what to fix these days," she said, turning back to the potatoes. "What with the high prices and rationing and shortages on top of that, it isn't easy."

Mom's younger than Dad, and her hair is darker brown than his and has less gray in it. Mom always dresses up for work because she says you have to look nice when you meet the public. She isn't really fat, but when she goes to church or to parties, she wears a girdle, only I'm not supposed to know that.

"You go for the paper now, Bobby," said Mom. "When you get back, the potatoes should be done." I took my time at the drugstore because Mom and Dad like to visit before dinner and talk about what they did that day and about family things.

Doc Delson's drugstore is at the end of the block and then across Central Avenue. It's on the corner in the row of stores with Heckman's butcher shop and Carlson's grocery store and Schultz's bakery. The drugstore is one of my favorite places. Doc doesn't care if you have a nickel to spend for a root beer or not. You're always welcome there. He even lets you read the comic books without buying.

Before Billy went into the air corps, he worked for Doc, jerking sodas and selling candy and cigarettes and magazines and things like that. Doc doesn't have anybody working there now, but he promised that when I'm older I can have a job. He pays thirty-five cents an hour and you get to eat all the ice cream you want.

Doc is a funny man and he'd rather be up front joking and talking with us kids and doing magic tricks for us, than mixing medicines in the back room. A lot of the grown-ups think he's peculiar because he's been to college, but he's as normal as anybody. Doc is short and bald and is always smiling. He wears glasses without rims and they're forever sliding down his nose and he keeps pushing them back up.

I paid Doc for the paper and climbed onto a stool at the soda fountain, right next to the display box of Ship Ahoy potato chips.

"Root beer, Bobby?" he asked.

"Naw, it's almost suppertime." And then I told him Billy was home.

"Saw him," he said, smiling. "He dropped by to say hello not twenty minutes ago."

"Tonight he's coming over to our house," I said. "He brought me something." A lady I didn't know came into the store with a prescription to be filled and Doc went to the back room.

I looked at the pictures in the new *Life* magazine, then went out and crossed Central Avenue and started running. But as I was passing our Victory Corner, I stopped for a look, like I almost always do. It's on the corner of our block, just kitty-corner from Doc's place, and right in front of the Gundersons' house. There's a Victory Corner on just about every block in Chicago.

Right in the middle of ours is the flagpole, and at its top we fly the American flag, of course, and just below it, our block's service flag. It's like the service flags you see in so many windows these days, except it's bigger. It has a wide red border around a field of white, and on the white is a blue star for every one of the boys on our block who is in the service. There are gold stars on it, too. Then we had two of them. One was for Stanley Schumm, who had been a sailor on the battleship USS Arizona, and was killed on December 7, 1941, when the Japs attacked Pearl Harbor. The other gold star is for the Kudalas' son, Myron, who had been a tank commander and was killed in action in North Africa.

In front of the flagpole is a large bulletin board, painted red, white, and blue, and covered with glass. On the left is a golden scroll that says "Our Roll of Honor" in fancy letters, and below it are the names of our servicemen. Billy's name is there, and so is my brother's. Next to the names of the boys who were killed in the war, there is a little gold star, like you get in Sunday school.

Pinned up around the honor roll are snapshots of most of our men in uniform. There's even a picture of Russ, taken in front of his barracks in Texas. He is wearing a big pack and helmet and is holding an M-1 rifle, which seems funny. He should be holding a typewriter instead, because Russ is a clerk-typist and has spent most of the war in Texas, typing something called morning reports. All of us are proud of him, though, because he enlisted and keeps volunteering to go overseas and fight, but they won't let him. They just keep him typewriting there in Texas and he hates it. There's a picture of Billy, too, taken right after he graduated from gunnery school. He's wearing a leather flight jacket and has his aerial gunner's wings pinned to it. The army-navy store up on Milwaukee Avenue near Irving Park Road had a jacket just like it in the window and I was saving up for it so I wouldn't have to wear Russell's old mackinaw another winter. Except the flight jacket was seventeen dollars and I had a long way to go. But, anyway, on that picture of Billy there's a big grin on his face, as usual, and his hat is cocked just the way it was when he got out of his uncle's car that very afternoon.

On the right side of the bulletin board are letters from our servicemen and announcements that Captain McGowan tacks up. His announcements tell about scrap drives and meetings and that sort of thing. When there's room he puts up posters telling us to buy war bonds and save kitchen fats, and not tell any military secrets. On his way to work every morning, Captain McGowan raises the flags and then he takes them down in the evening, on his way home. He is very dedicated.

I was reading a letter from Raymond Carlson, who is a marine stationed in the South Pacific, when I happened to remember supper. If I was late, Mom would have a fit because her meatloaf would dry up. I decided I'd read Raymond's letter another time, and ran home.

Chapter Five

THAT NIGHT SHIRLEY WASHED AND I DRIED. I hate doing dishes, but I have to. Mom says if I want to eat I've got to help in the kitchen.

Shirley was wearing blue jeans rolled up almost to the knees, and one of Russ's old dress shirts. It was big and baggy and she looked funny in it, but all the girls dress that way. We had finished the glasses and the plates and about half the silverware when the front doorbell rang. Mom and Dad were at the kitchen table, reading the paper.

★ 33 ★

"Who could that be?" asked Mom. We hardly ever have company after supper.

"Bet it's Billy," I said. "He told me he was coming over."

"*Bill!*" yelped Shirley. "Why didn't someone tell me?"

"You didn't ask," I said, and she gave me a dirty look as she untied her apron and stuffed it into the cabinet under the sink. She missed the hook and got it in the onion bin. "Just look at me!" she said. She ran from the kitchen and a second later I heard the bathroom door slam shut and then the click of the lock.

The doorbell rang again, and Dad said, *some*body had better answer it, by golly. Mom stood up, took off her own apron, and patted her hair with her fingertips and I put down the dish towel and hurried to the front door.

"I was beginning to think nobody was home," said Gunner. He laughed.

"C'mon in," I said. "We were just finishing the dishes." He took off his hat and put it on the table by the front door.

Mom and Dad came into the living room. Dad shook hands with Billy and said it was good to see him and welcomed him home. Mom put her arms around him and gave him a hug and kissed him, the way ladies do.

The four of us sat in the living room. Usually we sit in the kitchen at our house, or, if the weather's warm enough, we sit on the sun porch behind the kitchen. The living room is just for company, for special occasions. Billy coming home from overseas was a special occasion, all right.

"You look good, Billy," Mom told him, settling in her chair.

"A sight for sore eyes," said Dad. "How was the train ride?"

"Awful. It was hot and long and late and crowded."

"Oh, my, did you have to stand the whole way?" Mom asked.

"Just partway," he said.

Billy held a package on his lap and I was sure it was for me. I wanted to ask him if it was, but knew he'd think of it before long.

"You look thin," Mom said. "Isn't the army feeding you?" Mothers always think boys aren't eating the way they should. Billy chuckled and shrugged his shoulders and said he didn't know.

"Well, if I know your mother, she'll fatten you up while you're home, Billy," said Mom.

"Was it bad, son?" Dad asked, changing the subject. "Those missions?"

Billy leaned forward and for a second he looked thoughtful, and then he nodded. "Yeah—it was bad, real bad." His voice was so soft I had to strain to hear it.

"How many missions did you fly?"

"To finish our tour we needed thirty," he said, "but we ended up flying thirty-seven to make it. Seven missions didn't count. The brass only count the missions when you drop your bombs on target.

"A couple of times our targets were fogged in and we had to drop our load on the countryside. Another time we had oxygen trouble and had to quit the mission and make for England, quick as we could. And once," Gunner went on, "and please, don't tell Ma about this—a Nazi fighter jumped us and put out our number-three engine. We had to dump right there and limp home. I thought we'd had it, but we were lucky, because our squadron's fighter escort came along and scared off the Jerry bandit that had been pestering us. It was close."

"Oh, boy," I said softly. Mom bit her lower lip and shook her head, and Dad stared at the wall above Billy's head, as if watching for a distant Nazi fighter plane.

"Hey, what do you hear from my buddy, Russell?" asked Billy, trying to sound cheerful.

"A letter yesterday," said Mom.

"Is he liking Fort Sam Houston any better?"

"Not a bit," Dad laughed. "Fact, he tells us he hates every minute of it. Being there in San Antonio with all those soldiers and flyers from all the bases around there is worse than being on Guadalcanal in combat, he says."

"Well, I just thank the Lord he's *not* on Guadalcanal or some place where he could get hurt," Mom said. And suddenly she realized what she had said and was embarrassed.

"Sure," Billy said softly, to let her know he understood how mothers feel.

"Where do you go when your furlough's over?" Dad asked.

"Back to England," he said, "to fly a few more missions."

Mom frowned and said she was sorry.

"But I volunteered," said Billy. "Guess I could've pulled some Stateside duty for a while—a gunnery instructor, or something—but I'd like to be over there for the finish. This war can't go on a whole lot longer. I think those Germans have just about had it.

"With us bombing Germany by day with our '24s and

B-17s, and the British bombers hitting them 'most every night, why, it's got to be just a matter of time now."

It was exciting to hear about the war from somebody who had been in it, especially from Billy. We read about it in the papers and hear about it on the radio and see it in the newsreels when we go to the movies—still, it is hard to believe it's all actually happening. The war, I mean.

"Were you scared, Gunner?" I asked.

"Sure, Shadow, I was scared. Plenty. Every time I went up, I was scared. At first it was like a game—up there in formation with hundreds of other planes—but then, all of a sudden, it wasn't fun anymore. It was something we didn't want to do, but knew we *had* to do. Our outfit lost a couple of ships every mission— sometimes as many as one out of three. A lot of my close buddies went down. In the early morning at briefing before a mission, you'd look around at the other guys in the room and wonder who would get it that day—who wouldn't make it home for dinner.

"And it's selfish, I know, but you get to hoping and praying you'll be one of the lucky ones who *do* come back. You think it can't happen to you—it's always the other guys who get it." Billy leaned back in his chair and slowly shook his head.

"Every mission got worse. By the time we were up to twenty-three or twenty-four missions, we thought our luck was about due to run out, and every time we went up we knew the odds were a little more against us.

"Believe me, if you weren't much for praying before, you sure learned how, flying over Germany."

★ 37 ★

Mom and Dad and I all were sitting forward in our chairs, listening to every word Billy said. And suddenly he stopped.

"But, hey," he said, "I didn't come over here to make a patriotic speech. Let's talk about something happy."

So we all tried to think of something happy to say, but none of us could. Billy looked around the room, then asked if Shirley was out for the evening. He sounded disappointed.

"Naw," I said, "she's in the bathroom. She about lives in the bathroom."

Mom gave me a dirty look, and I knew I'd get it later. Dad chuckled and Billy's face got red. Then Gunner stood up, as if he was going to leave.

"Can I fix you something, Billy?" Mom asked. "Coffee or hot chocolate?"

"Not a thing, thanks," he said. "Way Ma fed me tonight, you'd have thought she was trying to fatten me up in one meal." Then he snapped his fingers.

"Almost forgot, Shadow," he said. "I've got something here for you," and he handed me the package he'd had under his arm. I undid the string and tore open the wrapping paper.

"Oh, boy—a model plane!"

"Not just a model plane," Billy said, pretending to sound hurt. "It's a B-24! Got it at the Post Exchange at our base in England."

It was a big, $2.49 model. I'd never tried to make one that big before. "It's swell, Gunner," I said. "It sure looks hard, though. Do you think you can help me while you're home?" He laughed and said he imagined he could work it into his schedule. And then I asked if he could come into my bedroom for a second.

"I've got something to show you, Gunner," I said.

"Sure," he said. "'Fraid I about wore out poor Ma and Pa over dinner with all I had to tell them. I expect they're both in bed by now."

Dad switched on the big living-room radio to see if he could find a news broadcast and Mom headed for the kitchen to finish the dishes and tidy up, and Billy and I went back to my bedroom.

I turned on the lamp and pointed to the wall, up next to the head of the bed.

"There," I said, and Billy moved in for a closer look. "It's my B-24 wall." There were pictures of B-24s that I had cut out of newspapers and magazines like *Life,* and there was a snapshot of Billy that I had taken with my Brownie the last time he was home on leave, just before he went overseas. He was wearing his flight jacket and was making a silly face and saluting at the camera. It isn't very good, but it was the best picture I had of him. It still is. Up next to it I had pinned the round Eighth Air Force insignia patch—like the one Billy had on the shoulder of his uniform. He had sent it to me right after he got to England.

"And when I finish the model, I'll hang it from the ceiling on threads, so it looks like it's flying," I said. I squinted my eyes and I could just see it swooping down out of the ceiling.

"That's some wall," Billy told me. "Glad to see you like the flyin' boxcar much as I do. A lot of people say it's too slow and awkward, but I'll take the Liberator over a '17 any day, or even over one of those new B-29s, for that matter."

"What's it like," I asked him. "I mean, back there in the tail where you are?"

"Oh, it's hard to explain. You're all alone, for one thing. Some of the guys—our navigator, Lieutenant Faulkner, especially—tease me about taking naps back there 'cause there's nobody to disturb me. But, believe me, Shadow, I'd never blink an eye back in the tail. Every second you've got to keep watching for those Jerry fighters."

Billy chuckled. "The sun shines through the Plexiglas and sometimes the guys on the crew call the tail the greenhouse, and they joke about my growing flowers back there.

"Truth is, there's hardly room for me, let alone a flowerpot."

"It's real crowded?"

"You said it! Why, if I was any bigger I'd have to smear myself with axle grease to squeeze into the tail.

"There's a little bicycle seat you perch on, and you've got your parachute on and the big guns there and you're wearing your life jacket and you're jammed in with the ammo cans and oxygen gear and the interphone and—well, you're just plain crowded. That's all there is to it."

To show how crowded it was, Billy sat down in the middle of my bedroom floor and hiked up his knees until they almost touched his chin. Then he hunched forward, with his head way down and his arms stretched between his cocked knees. With his index fingers stuck straight out, he said, "It's kind of like this, Shadow," and he frowned and went:

"Rat-tat-tat-tat. . . ."

"Well, hello, stranger," said a sickeningly sweet voice. *Shirley*. She was standing in the doorway to my bedroom and I have no idea how long she'd been watching us.

Poor Gunner. He got all flustered and his face turned seven shades of red, and he scrambled to his feet and stumbled over the ladder of my bunk bed and almost sprawled flat on his face.

"Hi, Shirl," he said, brushing the seat of his uniform pants with his hand.

"I heard you were home," Shirley said, trying to sound grown up.

"Yeah—this afternoon." Billy looked at Shirley from head to toe, then took another look. She had curled her hair and put on dark red lipstick that I knew belonged to Mom. She was wearing her best skirt and sweater, too, and bobby socks and her new saddle shoes that weren't even broken in yet.

"How've you been?" she asked, and he said okay and asked her how *she'd* been and she said she'd been okay, too.

"How's school?" She shrugged her shoulders and said it was okay. "But you know how school is. It just never changes."

Billy asked what classes she was taking and she said physics and English and public speaking and French and I forget what else.

"Oh," he said, and then he looked as though he was trying to think of something to say. Finally he did. "You're a senior?"

"Junior. I was three years behind you, Bill. Don't you remember?"

"I guess I do. It's just that you seem—you know, older. You look older."

I could have kicked Shirley. I wish I had. I wanted to hear Billy tell more about the war, not hear Shirley talk about school!

Shirley glanced into my dresser mirror and brushed at a curl with her fingertips, then sat sideways on my desk chair. Billy flopped onto my bed and leaned back on his elbows. I didn't know what to do, so I picked up the model he had brought me and sat cross-legged in the middle of the floor. Opening the end of the box, I dumped the stringers and the balsa sheets and the tube of glue and the rice paper and dope and everything else onto the floor in front of me and then I unfolded the plans. They were huge.

"Gosh, Gunner, this looks hard."

"You can handle it, buddy," he told me. "Otherwise, I wouldn't have brought it for you. Just take your time— don't try to rush it. You have any problems the next few weeks, I'll be right here to help."

Before I could answer, Shirley asked Billy how he liked being stationed in England. He liked it.

" 'Course, we didn't get off the base much, but once in a while we'd get into town," he said. "It's just a dinky little place called Horsham St. Faith. We'd eat fish and chips or go to the pub and drink an ale. Mostly, though, we just stayed on base and went to the Red Cross club or to the movies. Not very exciting."

"Did you like the English girls?" asked Shirley.

Billy's face got red. "They're okay, I guess," he said. "You just can't beat American girls, though."

I made a loud sigh and stuffed the plans and everything back into the box. Shirley reached over and turned on the radio and when it warmed up, tuned to a music station. *My* radio! Shirley got up and leaned over the bed and let her fingertips touch the rows of colored ribbons on Billy's uniform jacket.

"I know about your gunner's wings," she said, "but what do all these ribbons mean?"

Billy cleared his throat and started to tell her, but you could tell he didn't like it. He seemed real embarrassed. I had wondered about the ribbons, too, but hadn't wanted to ask.

One was the Distinguished Flying Cross, he said, and that was the most important one. He and the rest of his crew had gotten it because once, after a bomb run, they had stuck with another B-24 that had been hit and was limping back to England. They had helped fight off a couple of Nazi fighter planes that were trying to shoot down the crippled bomber. The blue ribbon with the golden orange stripe on each side stood for the Air Medal, and it was a decoration just about everybody in his outfit had received for flying all those missions. The one with all the different colors, he said, was the European Campaign Medal, and he got it, along with the two stars on it, "just for being there."

He hesitated and Shirley asked him to go on.

"Well, the other two aren't much," he said, clearing his throat. "The yellow one with red, white, and blue stripes on each end is the American Defense Service Medal, and anybody in uniform gets it. Even streetcar motormen and movie ushers." We all laughed.

"And here," he said, pointing to a red ribbon with white stripes on it, "is the one I got for behaving myself. It's the Good Conduct Medal."

"Oh, Bill," said Shirley, "I didn't realize you were a *hero*."

Gunner got redder'n a tomato.

"Heck, I'm sure not a hero," he said. "I'm just one of the lucky guys who made it back."

For what must have been at least a minute, neither of them said anything and I kept looking from Billy's face to Shirley's and back to Billy's again. They didn't so much as take their eyes off each other. Not for a second, they didn't.

"I—I thought about you a lot while I was over there," he said to her.

"And I thought a lot about *you*, too, Bill," she answered. Then Shirley reached out again and touched the silver wings and Billy's hand came up to her hand and quickly they both drew back, like they'd been burned. But in the second that they touched, I could almost see electricity or something—you know, like sparks—jump between them. I about gagged.

Shirley looked at him then and didn't say a word. Gunner tugged at his collar with a finger. It's pretty bad when a guy can't be in his own bedroom, but I wasn't staying in there another second. I went into the living room and stretched out on the floor in front of the radio. Mom and Dad were listening to "Duffy's Tavern," and it's not one of my favorite programs, but it's a lot better than Glenn Miller and all that gushy talk.

Mom was reading a story in the *Saturday Evening*

Post, and Dad sat with his head back on the chair, just relaxing. "What's the matter, little guy?" he asked. "Get chased out of your room?"

"You said it!" I told him, and he and Mom looked at each other and chuckled. I didn't see anything to laugh about, but you know parents. As I listened to the radio, I traced designs on the rug with my fingertip, and daydreamed about what it must be like to fly in a greenhouse at twenty-five thousand feet with a Jerry fighter coming at you.

It seemed so real, and when the plane got close enough I could see the Nazi pilot and he looked exactly like Shirley, only without my mom's lipstick. He had a mean smile on his face.

Chapter Six

LOVE SURE DOES WEIRD THINGS. IT HAD changed Gunner. Anybody could see that.

And love seems to happen all of a sudden, too, and there must not be anything you can do about it. With Gunner and Shirley it must've happened the very night he came home on furlough, because after that, he just wasn't himself at all. He didn't laugh and joke and monkey around the way he used to.

Just looking at them, you could tell they were in love.

When they were together, Shirley always got that same look on her face that she gets when she eats something that doesn't agree with her and she gets sick to her stomach. Dad says when a girl looks like that it means she's in love. I didn't get too close to her, though, because if she was sick I didn't want her to throw up on me. I wasn't taking any chances.

Every time I turned around that whole month of October, they were together, talking. Probably they talked plenty of other times, when I wasn't around to see them. I can't imagine what they talked about so much, because Shirley doesn't know a thing about airplanes or softball or the war or anything. I've known her all my life and she never has anything interesting to say.

At home Shirley acted strange, like she was day-dreaming. It was enough to make a person want to go into the bathroom and heave. Except that Shirley was almost always in there curling her hair or putting on lipstick or looking for pimples, so you couldn't throw up even if you wanted to.

It used to be, before Billy went off to war, that he was fun to be with. We did things together and had some swell times. Like the time we helped out together when our block's Victory Corner was being dedicated. Believe me, that was really something. Mr. Koontz had been acting up that day, and it was a cinch we wouldn't have an easy time of it getting him up on that roof.

"No, siree, boys, I ain't gonna do it an' *that* is *that!*" said Mr. Koontz, his face all wrinkled up in a frown and his jaw set, like he meant what he said. "You'll just have to find yourself another bugler!"

With that, Mr. Koontz sat down on the Gundersons' back steps and crossed his arms over his chest and frowned harder. He was some sight, sitting there in his old Spanish-American War uniform.

Mr. Koontz had been a Rough Rider with Teddy Roosevelt, and when it was new, his uniform must have looked just like the one Teddy is wearing in those pictures in the history books. Now it's almost all patched and mended over. The jacket and pants are faded brown canvas, and the leggings are canvas, too. Under his coat he wears a flannel shirt that is so light blue it must've been washed ten thousand times.

Every Memorial Day and Armistice Day, Mr. Koontz wears that old uniform, and he wears it on the Fourth of July, too. On the Sunday the Japs attacked Pearl Harbor, he put it on and went up to the corner of Central Avenue and Addison Street and marched right into Yick Yee's carryout chop suey place and demanded that Yick Yee surrender to him. Mr. Haugen, who is Ralph's father, was in there getting a quart of chicken chow mein and an order of egg foo yung and a half-dozen almond cookies for Sunday dinner. He saw the whole thing and he told Ralph about it and Ralph told me and the other guys. Anyway, Mr. Koontz called Yick Yee a dirty Jap and he started swinging a two-by-four he had brought from home, and Yick Yee got his meat cleaver from the kitchen and he waved it at Mr. Koontz and hollered back that he was a Chinaman, not a Jap! They stood yelling at each other and Mr. Haugen ran outside and pulled the lever on the fire alarm box at the corner.

The firemen kept Mr. Koontz and Yick Yee apart until

the cops got there. The police drove Mr. Koontz home in the paddy wagon and Mrs. Koontz was mortified. Right after that, Yick Yee put a big American flag in his front window, along with a picture of Chiang Kai-shek and a sign that said he was Chinese.

"But you promised you'd blow the bugle for the dedication," argued Billy that afternoon in the Gundersons' backyard. "Come on, Mr. Koontz, you can't let us down."

"Think of our boys overseas, fighting to defend us," I said, "just like you did in the Spanish-American War."

For a second Mr. Koontz straightened his shoulders, like he was trying to push out his chest, but he shook his head and said, "Nope."

"But, why not, Mr. Koontz?" said Billy. "Tell us why you won't do it."

Hefting the short, stubby old bugle that was all dented and scratched, the old man looked at it and shook his head. "Don't ask me that, sonny," he said quietly.

Billy and I looked at each other and he shrugged. If we didn't get Mr. Koontz up there on that roof pretty quick, we'd all be in trouble. Dedicating that block Victory Corner was important, and if Mr. Koontz wouldn't blow his bugle, the dedication would be ruined.

It was all Captain McGowan's idea. As block captain he was in charge of the dedication, too. Before we got into the war and the neighbors elected him our block captain, he used to walk just like regular men. But since he got elected, he's been *marching*. Captain McGowan marches everywhere he goes.

When he is on Civil Defense business and has to call on

everybody about war bonds or kitchen fats or ration coupons or something, he puts on his big white Civil Defense helmet and marches from door to door. On his way to work every morning, he marches to the Victory Corner flagpole, raises the flags, then marches on to the bus stop, and in the evenings he marches home from it. And he marches to the drugstore and to the bakery and to church on Sunday and to Vito's tavern and I suppose he marches around inside his house, too.

Captain McGowan isn't much taller than I am, and he wears thick eyeglasses that he has to squint to see through, and he has a funny little mustache with waxed tips that must tickle Mrs. McGowan when he kisses her. He always wears a suit and a necktie, and none of the other men do that except on Sundays, when they go to church. But he has to doll up because he works downtown at Marshall Field's department store.

"I work in ladies' shoes," he tells everybody, and whenever I hear him say that I almost laugh out loud, because I can just imagine him wearing a pair of high-heeled shoes, like Mom wears, and marching up and down the Marshall Field's aisles.

Anyway, getting Mr. Koontz up onto the Gundersons' roof was his idea. Captain McGowan thought it would be very dramatic to have the bugler up there. Sometimes he has peculiar ideas. The captain had first wanted to have the drum and bugle corps from the American Legion post over on Diversey Street play for our honor roll dedication, but they were booked solid on Sunday afternoons for the next six months.

When he couldn't get the drum and bugle corps,

Captain McGowan settled for Mr. Koontz and Mrs. Zielinski. She lives in the nice brick house across the alley from us, and she plays the accordion. She is so good she plays for weddings and for dances and parties, and once she was on the radio with nine other ladies, all playing the accordion at once. You should have heard it. The only trouble is, everything Mrs. Zielinski plays sounds like a polka.

I had been looking forward to the dedication because right afterward there was going to be a block party in the McGowans' basement. Our block parties are always fun because Juicy and Ralph and Ed and I and a couple of other guys always get to messing around. All the women in the neighborhood cook and bake things, and even with shortages and rationing, they put on a swell feed. You can go back to the table as many times as you want to, and nobody says anything.

And Mrs. Zielinski always brings her accordion to the block parties, and after the meeting and meal, she plays polkas and the grown-ups dance and us kids fool around. The McGowans have the nicest basement I've ever seen. The walls are painted and so is the floor, and they have war posters and *Saturday Evening Post* covers hanging up all over. They even have an extra toilet in the basement.

Anyway, for the dedication, our alderman would make some inspirational remarks and a Catholic priest and a Lutheran minister would tend to all the praying. Captain McGowan had tried to get a real war hero to make the main speech, but he couldn't find one, so he decided to make a patriotic speech himself. Between all the speeches and prayers, Mrs. Zielinski would offer what Captain McGowan called "incidental patriotic music." I hated to think of standing still through all of that. But Billy rescued me from it when he asked me to help him with Mr. Koontz. The captain had put Billy in charge of Mr. Koontz and I would be Billy's assistant.

That might not sound like much of a job, but believe me, it sure was. Mr. Koontz has a mind of his own and he might or might not do something when people ask him to. That afternoon of the dedication he was in one of his "might not" moods.

So he said again that he wouldn't set foot on that roof and didn't want to hear another word about it. He put the horn on the step beside him and tugged his uniform hat down hard on his head.

I peeked around the side of the house and there must've been more than a hundred people out there in front, all gathered around the flagpole. Captain McGowan, wearing his white Civil Defense helmet, climbed up onto the little platform they had built for the speakers, and he blew twice into the microphone he had borrowed from his lodge, and he said, "Is this thing working?" and his voice blasted through the loud-speaker. Everybody hollered back, "*Yes!*" and he raised his arms in the air for quiet.

The captain looked around and saw that everybody was ready, so he nodded to Mrs. Zielinski. Then Mr. Zielinski and the alderman helped her up onto the platform. With her and her accordion up there, there wasn't room for the block captain, and he had to step down and stand to one side. He looked peeved about it because he is so short nobody could see him in the crowd.

Mrs. Zielinski flashed that big smile she always has when she plays her accordion, then she bobbed her head, tapped her foot, and started playing our national anthem. She played it better than I've ever heard her play it before except that it sounded like the "Star-Spangled Banner Polka." She sure puts a whole lot into her music.

I hurried to the back of the house and Billy was still trying to make Mr. Koontz climb that ladder.

Mr. Koontz shook his head. "All right, boys, I'll tell you. I got no choice," said the old man as he picked up the bugle and drummed his fingernails on it. "It's my teeth.

"A year ago I had all my God-given teeth pulled an' ever since, I can't blow this here horn worth a dang," he said. "Anymore, I play this thing an' it sounds like an ol' milk cow blowin' a fart."

"Oh, boy, Mr. Koontz," said Billy. "Why didn't you tell that to Captain McGowan?"

The old man clacked his teeth to show that they were store-bought and said, "Wasn't none of that pipsqueak's business!"

Billy nodded that he understood, and jammed his hands deep into his pants pockets and frowned. Then he scratched his head and bit his lip, like he was thinking hard. I scratched my head and bit my lip, too, but it didn't help at all. I didn't get any bright ideas. One of us would just have to go up to the platform and whisper to Captain McGowan that Mrs. Zielinski would have to play taps on the accordion and that was that.

All at once Billy snapped his fingers and grinned. "Got it," he said. "Shadow, you know how to play taps—I've heard you a hundred times. You—"

"Not on your life!" I said, quick as I could. "I ain't going to put on Mr. Koontz's uniform and stand up there on the roof in front of all those people and play that bugle. No, sir, Billy!"

My brother Russ had been in the Boy Scouts with Billy, and Russ got to be troop bugler. He even bought his own bugle from a mail order ad in *Boy's Life*, and sometimes he'd let me mess around with it. I got so I could play the cavalry charge, like in the movies, and taps.

"Shadow, you don't have to stand in front of all those people," said Billy. He stopped talking and raised his hand to cock an ear at what was happening in front of the house. Mrs. Zielinski was playing the air corps' "Wild Blue Yonder Polka." Time was running out.

"C'mon, now, Shadow," Billy argued. "Mr. Koontz can stand at the peak of the roof in his uniform, so everybody sees him, and he'll pretend he's playing his bugle, only it'll really be *you* blowing Russ's bugle, hiding behind the chimney where nobody can see you."

I bit my lip and shook my head. I didn't know what to say.

"You run home and get Russ's bugle, Shadow, and I'll help Mr. Koontz get up onto the roof."

I looked at Mr. Koontz standing at attention in his old uniform. He turned his head and nodded to show he liked Billy's plan. Then he smiled, but his false teeth slipped and he shut his mouth quickly.

"Gee whiz," I said.

"There's no time for gee-whizzin'," said Billy. "Hop on your horse and get that blasted horn!"

I shrugged an okay, even though I didn't like it one

bit. I ran out of the Gundersons' back gate and through the alley to our house. We live just four houses away, so it didn't take a second. From our backyard I could see Mr. Koontz halfway up that wobbly ladder with Billy right behind him. They were moving slowly. I was in and out of the house in about three seconds flat, and on my way back to the Gundersons' yard. I was in such a hurry to scramble up to the roof that I got a sliver in my hand from that old wooden ladder, but there wasn't time for first aid. I laughed to myself. Maybe they'd give me a Purple Heart Medal, since I got the splinter in service to my country. At least to my block.

From the Gundersons' roof you can see all the way to Portage Park, which is straight up Central Avenue, just across Irving Park Boulevard. That's about five blocks away. As long as I could remember, there had been a big old World War I cannon at the entrance to Portage Park, and us kids used to climb all over it and play soldiers. But right after the Japanese attacked Pearl Harbor, the cannon was hauled away to be melted down to make new cannons to fight the Japs and Nazis. Now there's just a big empty cement platform where the cannon used to be.

Up there on the roof, I wasn't feeling at all good. It had been a long time since I had played taps, and always before when I had played it, it had been just fooling around. I hated to recite in school or say a piece in church, and playing a bugle for a lot of people was worse, even though they wouldn't see me. I was scared about that, and the roof was slanty and a couple of times my gym shoes started to slip and I was scared about that, too. I don't know whether I was more afraid of blowing the bugle or falling off the roof.

★ 55 ★

The cars and trucks and trolley buses were moving right along on Central Avenue. Once in a while, someone would honk a car horn at the people gathered around the Victory Corner, almost like a salute. Across Central Doc Delson stood out in front of his drugstore, leaning against the mailbox on the corner. When he saw me on the roof he waved and I waved back. You sure can see a lot from the Gundersons' roof. More than from ours.

I scrunched down behind the chimney, and Mr. Koontz and Billy were up at the peak of the roof. When it was time, Billy helped the trumpeter to his feet. Mr. Koontz looked shaky, and his knees wobbled, and Billy crouched behind him to catch him in case he started to fall, but he didn't.

The Lutheran minister was saying the closing prayer then, and even though I could hear his voice, I didn't understand the words. I saw Mr. Koontz stand straighter and lift his stubby, dented horn to his lips, and I raised Russ's Boy Scout bugle to mine. Then Billy gave me the signal. I was shaking like a leaf, but I took a deep breath, wet my lips real good, and blew.

Day is done, gone the sun, from the hill, from the lake, from the sky; All is well, safely rest, God is nigh. . . .

I held onto that last note long as I could and let it fade, then, until it was nothing. I felt my face getting red. And then it was over. I got through it okay, but never again would I do that, no matter what Billy or anybody else said. I didn't make any mistakes, except near the end I ran out of breath and had to sneak in an extra puff. When I finished, Billy was all smiles, and he made the okay sign.

★ 56 ★

"Tolerable job you done, sonny," Mr. Koontz said, when we were back on the ground. "'Course, you're gonna have to work on your breathin' some, and practice, if you're gonna be a trumpeter like me someday."

At first I was mad at the old man, because I thought I had blown pretty well, but then I saw that he had tears in his eyes, so I didn't say anything to him about it. I knew he must be sorry he hadn't been able to do it himself.

Billy patted me on the back. "Thanks, Shadow. That was a swell job, buddy. You saved the day!"

That's what I mean about Billy. About the way he used to be. But that October when he came home on furlough, he was different. Gunner had changed because he was in love.

Darn that Shirley, anyway.

Chapter Seven

YOU COULDN'T JUST LOOK AT BILLY AND SEE that he was different. It wasn't like that at all. It wasn't as if he had grown a bushy red beard or something like that. At first I just thought he was being polite to Shirley, even though he was sort of overdoing it. How was I to know he was in love with her?

The day after he came home I finished all my Saturday chores as fast as I could and got to work on the B-24. I started with the left side of the fuselage. When you get the frame of the two sides done, you join them with short

★ 58 ★

pieces of balsa wood and then you put—well, you know how to make a model.

I had to quit working on the plane to eat supper, but soon as dishes were done and the kitchen was cleaned up, I went back into my room and got to work on it again. I was excited about the B-24, and I could hardly wait to get it finished and hanging from the ceiling. For a while things went okay, but then I started having troubles. That always happens to me. I wished Billy would come over and help. I hadn't seen him all day and didn't even know if he was home. I went to the living room and looked next door. I was in luck—there was Billy, sitting on the front steps with his father. I hurried out, before he could go inside.

"Hi, Mr. Eckert," I said to Billy's dad. "I haven't seen you for a long time."

"Been thinking that myself, Robert," said Mr. Eckert. "Just where have you been keeping yourself?"

"Gosh, I haven't been keeping myself anyplace, sir— just around here, like always. Must be you who's keeping himself someplace."

Mr. Eckert is a little man, even shorter than Billy, and he has wide shoulders and is almost bald. His nose is too big for the rest of his face, and he has droopy eyes. Billy sure doesn't get his good looks from him. Or his mother, either. His good looks must've been a mistake. Mr. Eckert is nice, though. He'd have to be, to have a son like Billy.

"Hi, Shadow," Gunner said. "I keep telling Pa he should take things easier, and stay around the house once in a while, but he thinks we can't win the war unless he puts in all that overtime at the plant."

Mr. Eckert chuckled and then stood up and stretched and said he'd better be turning in. He told us good night and went into the house. I sat next to Billy and he asked me what I was up to.

"Working on that model," I said, "and it's tough. In fact, I just got started and I'm stuck already."

"Can I give you a hand?"

"Would you? That'd be swell, because I can't go any further until I get some help."

"Let me tell Ma, Shadow," he said, mussing my hair. "I'll be over in a jiffy."

Mom and Dad were in the kitchen reading the paper and talking.

"Billy's coming to help me with the model."

"Maybe you shouldn't pester him so much, little guy," said Dad, looking up from the funnies. "I expect Harold and Naomi would like to see more of him."

"They were going to bed," I said. "At least his father was. And besides, it was Billy's idea. He asked if he could help me."

"And of course you said he could."

"Of course," I answered, and Mom and Dad looked at each other and smiled.

Shirley's door was closed and I could hear music coming from her bedroom. I went to the front door and opened it and waited there so Gunner wouldn't have to ring the doorbell. Then Shirley would never know Billy was in the house. Before long he came up the steps, two at a time. He had put on a clean sport shirt and slacks. He had brushed his hair, too, and he smelled of Old Spice shaving lotion. He didn't have to go and fix himself up like that just to work on the model, but I guess you get in the habit of being neat in the air corps.

We were walking through the living room and I was being quiet as I could, when Shirley's door opened and she came out. I could've kicked her.

"Why, Bill," she said, "what a surprise!" She makes me sick the way she tries to sound so grown up. "What brings you over?"

"Your brother brings me over," he said. "I'm going to give him a hand with his model plane."

The three of us went into the kitchen and Billy talked with my folks for a minute; then he and I went into my bedroom. I shut the door right behind me before Shirley could follow us in.

For about twenty minutes Billy and I worked on the plane, and it wasn't long before he had me pretty well straightened out. I had been doing it all wrong, only he didn't come right out and say that. He just showed me a better way to pin those long stringers, so that they wouldn't split. And he taught me how to cut the cross-pieces so they'd be the exact size, instead of being too short or too long, the way they always are when I do it myself. We had begun to glue the crosspieces into place when my bedroom door flew open. Shirley!

"Didn't anyone ever teach you how to knock?" I said. I was really mad and that's what she always says to me when I go into her bedroom, which I hardly ever do.

"I'm sorry, *Mis*-ter Simpson," she said in her snottiest voice, "but I thought maybe Bill would like to hear 'Your Hit Parade.' It's coming on now, and I've made cocoa."

"Your Hit Parade" is the worst program they put on

the radio. All it is is music. They play the ten songs that are most popular each week, and they try to make it seem as though it's the most important thing there is. Even more important than the war.

"I'd like that," Gunner said. I was shocked. I couldn't imagine Billy ever wanting to listen to a program like that. "Shadow and I were just finishing up here—he's got the hang of it now."

I could hear the music coming from the living room. Shirley left my bedroom and went into the kitchen, where she picked up a tray with two cups of hot chocolate on it. She started out of the kitchen, then stopped. "Yours is on the stove," she said to me over her shoulder, and she turned and led Billy into the front room.

"Thanks a lot," I called after her. I sat with Mom and Dad, who were drinking hot chocolate, too, and Mom said I shouldn't be so sarcastic. Then she told me to hurry and drink mine so I could get into that bathtub.

"But why does she get to stay up—"

"She's older, little guy," said Dad.

"But I don't even need a bath," I said, between sips. "I haven't done anything all week to get dirty."

Mom laughed like that was the funniest thing she had heard in years. "Just hurry on in and scrub well—you're filthy!"

I grabbed my clean pj's from the dresser and shoved the drawer shut. Then I went into the bathroom and slammed the door loud as I could. As I brushed my teeth, I made faces at myself in the mirror, then rinsed toothpaste from my mouth, started the bathwater running in the tub, and undressed.

And I kept thinking every second about Shirley sitting out there in the living room listening to "Your Hit Parade," and drinking cocoa with Billy. And her acting real stuck-up like she was twenty-some years old, instead of only seventeen, and poor Billy having to smile and act polite to her.

I made a long, loud raspberry noise that nobody could hear but me, and climbed into the tub. Dad is always telling me I should enjoy myself and have fun because being a kid is the best time of life.

That doesn't make any sense at all, because the only thing I ever get to do is go to school and do chores and take baths and that isn't any fun at all. I started washing my face and got soap in my eyes and it stung like anything!

I was so mad I slapped my hand flat on the water and a lot splashed out of the tub all over the floor.

Now I had to wipe *that* up before I went to bed.

And Dad says it's so great being a kid! He must've forgotten how it really is.

Chapter Eight

THOSE DAYS OF OCTOBER THAT GUNNER WAS
home on furlough passed quickly.

The World Series came and went. The St. Louis Cards
and the St. Louis Browns played for six days straight
and every afternoon, after school, you heard the game on
the radio no matter where you went. I'm not much of a
baseball fan, but everybody was listening to it, it
seemed. You couldn't get away from it. The Browns won
the first and third games. The Cardinals took the second

game and then swept the last three to take the series, four games to two. Most of the real good players were in the service and the big league teams had mostly young guys and old men and players who had something wrong with them, so they couldn't get into the army or navy to fight. The Browns even had an outfielder named Pete Gray, who had only one arm.

There was plenty to keep me busy with school and chores and with collecting scrap paper and tin cans and things for the war effort. Sometimes when I listened to the radio at night, I worked on the model.

Billy kept busy, too, and I saw him sometimes, but not as much as you would've thought. He and Shirley were together a lot and I guess that's because they were in love. They talked plenty—it seemed they were always talking—and they took long walks in the chilly October evenings. Sometimes I saw them holding hands, and probably when nobody else was around they kissed.

The weather was getting cooler and I had to wear a sweater to school. More and more leaves fell so there was always raking to be done.

One afternoon I was raking the yard and Gunner came out of his house and he hopped the fence and sat on our back steps. We talked.

"Thursday's Columbus Day," I said. "No school—I can hardly wait!" I was hoping he would suggest we do something together, but he didn't. I had to.

"You think maybe we could go downtown to the Field Museum?"

"Golly, Shadow, I'd really like to," he said. "Wish you'd mentioned it sooner, but I already asked Shirley to go downtown to the show. There's a Spencer Tracy picture at the Chicago Theater, and Perry Como's on stage in person."

"Okay," I said. "I just thought I'd ask." If he wanted to go to the show with Shirley and listen to some guy sing mushy love songs, instead of seeing all those swell mummies and Indian things, that was his business. I kept right on raking and didn't say another word.

So I spent Columbus Day with Juicy instead of Gunner. We had our mothers pack lunches for us and early in the morning we took the bus downtown. We decided to go to the Rosenwald Museum, instead of the Field Museum. The Rosenwald Museum is very educational, but it's fun, too. Miss Connelly gives you extra credit, just for going.

They have a coal mine right there in the museum. It's not real, but it sure seems like it is. When I was little I used to think it was scary. And they have an old-time town in the museum, with old-fashioned stores and streets and real autos and a movie house that shows silent pictures for a nickel. The best thing, though, is the appendix operation. When you look at it, it makes you feel like you have a pain in your right side, it's so real.

They have models of somebody's middle—Juicy said they are made of plaster—behind glass, and you go from one to the next and you get to see how a doctor cuts out your appendix. All life-size. You see the guts hanging out and the blood and everything. It's enough to make you sick. I could only go through it two times, from start to finish, where the doctor sews you up. Juicy went back six times.

Riding home on the bus, Juicy said he was going to be a doctor when he grows up, because it must be fun to cut somebody apart like that. His mother is real good at sewing, he said, so she could teach him how to sew up somebody and he wouldn't have to go to doctor school so long. He hates school.

"Nuts, not me," I said. "If you have to do stuff like cutting open somebody's belly to get at the appendix, with blood squirting all over the place, I sure don't want to be a doctor!" Juicy laughed at me. He doesn't mind seeing blood and all. Once he even told me he would like to be an undertaker because his dad says they make lots of money. Not me. I'd rather be poor than do that.

Downtown where we changed buses it seemed almost half the people we saw were soldiers and sailors and marines and all in uniform. In Chicago the servicemen get treated real well. There are special clubs for them called canteens and they get food and see free shows and can dance there, And, besides, they can get into the movies here for half price and they can ride on the buses and streetcars free.

When we got home it was still afternoon, so we got up a game of softball. Ralph and Ed played and so did Norman, the new kid who lives over on Grace Street.

Even though it was football season, we played softball. It used to be we'd sometimes play touch tackle in the street in the fall, but last year a delivery truck ran over Ralph's football and we haven't played football since. So we play softball all year, except when it's too cold or there's snow or ice on the street.

We hardly ever have enough guys to play sides, so

mostly we play piggy-move-up. Kids have been playing softball on Warwick Avenue for years. It's boys only. All the girls play jump rope with an old clothesline on the sidewalk in front of Fern's house. We never pay any attention to them and they pretend we aren't there.

Anyway, that Columbus Day after Juicy and I got home from the Rosenwald Museum, we were playing ball, and who should walk out of his house but Billy. He sat on the curb next to the fireplug in front of the Albachs' house.

"How's chances of a guy gettin' in the game?" Billy asked after a while. We told him sure, but he'd have to start in the outfield where new players always have to start.

I was pitching then. "Good movie," he said as he passed me on his way to the outfield. "All about a guy who escaped from a Nazi concentration camp. You'd have liked it, Shadow."

Juicy told him we'd gone to the Rosenwald Museum and had seen a real, honest-to-God appendix operation. I'd have lots rather seen the Spencer Tracy movie than the appendix operation, only I didn't say so.

It was a good game. It seemed like just having Billy there made all of us play better than usual. Ralph was having trouble hitting the ball, and Billy had moved up to pitch to him. He called time out and went to the plate.

"If you turn your left shoulder more toward the pitcher, you'll get a better swing," Billy told him, and he turned Ralph by the shoulders, to show him. "And hunch over more—and keep the bat off your shoulder and your eye on the ball."

Ralph did exactly what Gunner said and hit a triple. Next time up, though, he forgot everything Billy had taught him and went back to his old way of batting and struck out.

If he'd wanted to, Billy could have stayed up at bat until his furlough was over, just hitting one homer after another. But he didn't put anywhere near everything into his swing, and he had a couple of pretty good hits, but nothing special. Nothing like the way he used to hit when I was little and sat on the curb and watched. Out in the field, he even dropped an easy pop fly Norman had hit and Norman took second.

"C'mon, Gunner," I hollered once, "take a real swing at it! You're not half trying!"

Gunner smiled and said he guessed he was out of shape because he hadn't played since he left home. "And you get a little rusty just sittin' around the barracks all the time," he added.

But I knew that wasn't true. He wasn't rusty at all. It was just Gunner's way. He knew he could hit and pitch and field better than any of the rest of us, but he just didn't want to seem too good.

Before long Juicy's mom hollered for him to get home, and Ralph and Ed said they'd better go, too, so the game was over. Norman drifted off without even saying good-bye. He's strange.

Billy and I sat on the curb by the fireplug. "Enjoying your leave?" I asked him. He said he was.

"I'm afraid I'm not going to want to go back," he said. "I'm getting spoiled, with home-cooked food, sleeping late, no missions. It's the life."

"But you have to go back, don't you?"

"Afraid so, Shadow. But I dread those missions like anything. Getting hauled out of bed at three o'clock in the morning, shivering in the cold, sitting through briefing and breakfast and then going out to the ships. It's cold and foggy and we sit there in the planes, waiting, drinking coffee, hoping to hear the mission is scrubbed because of bad weather, or something. Usually it's the fog that keeps us there and we sit and wait for it to lift.

"Sometimes we wait for two hours and they call it off, and that's as bad as flying the mission, because you've spent all that time getting ready for it. It's a letdown.

"But then," said Billy, "when you do fly, you're forever looking for those Jerry bandits to come at you from out of nowhere, angling for a shot. And when you near the target there's the antiaircraft fire to worry about.

"Once in a while, especially over a big target, it seems those bursts of flak are so thick you could get out of the plane and walk on them, stepping from one to the next."

"Gee, Gunner," I said in a soft voice, "I wish you didn't have to go back. I wish you could just stay home, like before."

"Wish so, too, Shadow, but we've got to get this war over with before the guys your age have to get into it."

For a time Gunner looked like he was thinking real hard, sitting there with his knees up and his arms crossed over them and his chin resting on his arms.

"But it won't be long," he said. "I've got this feeling that the war's going to be over before we know it, and I'll be home for good."

"I hope you're right," I said. "What are you going to do then, Billy? After the war, I mean."

"College, I guess. Maybe study engineering, maybe math. I'll see when the time comes." For a minute he was quiet again, and then he asked how I was getting along with the B-24.

"Got the fuselage about finished last night and now I'm ready to get going on the wings. Tonight, probably."

"If I have a chance I'll stop by and have a look at it."

"Swell, Gunner."

Then, without either of us saying anything more, we stood up and walked toward our houses. Billy laid an arm over my shoulder and we walked slowly. I kicked at a stone on the sidewalk, and when we came to it again, Billy gave it a kick and it went out into the street.

At his front sidewalk he squeezed my shoulder, said, "See ya, Shadow," and turned off to go inside.

"See ya, Gunner," I answered. I walked on alone, slowly, and cut across the grass toward the backyard gate.

I felt good and I started whistling.

Chapter Nine

I WAS AT SCHOOL THE MONDAY MORNING MR. Koontz fell off the toilet and broke his hip, so I missed all the excitement. I always do. Just like the time Mrs. Ohlson had the big fight with Mr. Heckman. I missed that, too. She's the Baptist and he's the butcher, and she got real mad one time about the un-Christian sign he put in the window of his shop.

Usually his signs say something like, "BROILERS— 39¢ LB.," and there isn't anything un-Christian about that. What got Mrs. Ohlson so mad was when Mr. Heckman put a sign in the window that said, "LADIES— GET YOUR FAT CANS IN HERE!" Most people knew he was joking about saving kitchen fats for the war effort and thought his sign was funny. But not everybody.

Mrs. Ohlson told Mr. Heckman she didn't think the sign was one bit funny and he said something to her that wasn't very nice and before anybody knew what was happening, she hit him with her umbrella on the straw hat he always wears and finally it took Doc Delson and Reverend Oakley, the Baptist preacher, to make peace. She said the sign was sinful and he said, phooey, that it was just a joke and that folks needed something to laugh about in wartime. Finally Mr. Heckman took the sign down, but to this day Mrs. Ohlson won't set foot in his shop. I missed that excitement, too, and Doc had to tell me all about it.

Anyway, it was a shame about Mr. Koontz. He's the old Spanish-American War bugler who pretended to play taps from the roof of the Gundersons' house. It was lucky he fell off the toilet instead of the Gundersons' roof, or he'd have broken more than just his hip.

Mrs. Zielinski told me about Mr. Koontz's accident that day after school. I had gone across the alley to her house to help clean the garage. She had lots of old magazines she had decided to give me for the scrap-paper drive. Besides that, Mrs. Zielinski said she'd pay me a dollar for helping her and I could sure use that money for my flight jacket.

When I saw how many magazines there were in the garage, I almost fell over. Half of one wall was stacked with *Life* and *Collier's* and *Saturday Evening Post* and *Liberty* magazines, all going way back. There was hardly room for their Buick in the garage. I'd never be able to get all those magazines to school in my dumb little wagon.

Mrs. Zielinski was wearing an apron over her house-dress and she had on a sweater because it was chilly. The garage doors were open and she stood outside, looking at all the magazines and shaking her head. She held her sweater at her throat.

"They're almost like dear, old friends, those magazines are," she said. "So many wonderful stories, so many hours of good reading. It's a shame to give them up, but if it'll help the war effort. . . ." I was afraid she was going to cry.

We got right to work and it went fast. Once she stopped and went into the house and brought out a big plate of cookies. She put the plate on the hood of the Buick and every now and then we'd stop and eat a cookie.

"Pity about poor Mr. Koontz," she said, when we were almost finished tying up bundles of magazines.

"What do you mean?" I said.

"You hadn't heard? He fell off the toilet and broke his hip, poor dear."

"Off the *toilet?*" I sat down on the running board of the car and looked at her.

"Oh, no," said Mrs. Zielinski, and she smiled. "Mr. Koontz wasn't sitting—he was *standing* on the toilet, changing the light bulb in the bathroom. Lost his balance and toppled over. Hit the tub, then the floor.

"Poor Mrs. Koontz called the fire department."

Mrs. Zielinski shook her head. "They say he was hurting something awful. The firemen got there and called an ambulance and it took him out to the Veterans Hospital. Be in there for some while, I expect."

"Gee," I said. "An ambulance and a fire engine on our block and I wasn't even home to see it." And then I realized how mean that must've sounded, and I added, "I sure hope Mr. Koontz gets okay soon."

"We all do," said Mrs. Zielinski, touching my shoulder. "But only time will tell." For a second she didn't say anything. Maybe she was thinking about the day the Victory Corner was dedicated. That's what I was thinking of.

"Here—have this last cookie, Robert," she said, "and we'll finish bundling those magazines."

Just as I was knotting the last bundle, Gunner came up to the open door.

"You're too late, William. Robert just ate the last cookie," Mrs. Zielinski said.

"Hey, Gunner," I said. "Did you hear about Mr. Koontz?"

"Doc told me," he said, nodding.

"What did Mr. Delson say?" asked Mrs. Zielinski, crossing her arms. Billy leaned against the fender of the Buick.

"Doc says, with a person that age, a broken hip can be serious," said Billy. "He said bones are brittle and slow to mend, and then there are all kinds of complications."

Being a druggist, Doc knows plenty about medicine. In our neighborhood, when somebody gets sick they don't go to a doctor right away unless they fall off a toilet and break a hip or something. What they do is go see Doc Delson and tell him where it hurts.

"I'm not a doctor," he always says, "but if it was me, had a pain like that, I'd try some of these pills, and if they didn't help, I'd go right down and see my doctor."

Usually the pills he sells you help. So hardly anybody in our neighborhood ever has to see a doctor. Just Doc Delson. I'll bet Doc could even take out somebody's appendix, like at the Rosenwald Museum.

"Well, we can all pray that Mr. Koontz mends quickly," said Mrs. Zielinski. Billy said, "Yes'm," but I didn't say anything. I just nodded.

"What's the matter?" Billy asked me. "Looks like something's bugging you."

"I'm trying to figure out how to get all these magazines to school tomorrow morning," I said. "Be about ten loads in the wagon."

For a second Billy looked thoughtful. Then he said he figured he could help me.

"Let's load 'em into Pa's car and I'll drive you and them to school in the morning. Since it's for the war effort, I know Pa'll say it's okay."

"Gosh, Gunner, that'll be swell." I could hardly wait until morning.

Mrs. Zielinski watched while Billy and I went back and forth between her garage and Billy's, carrying bundles of magazines. It almost seemed like we were taking away all those old friends of hers.

When we were done she took a dollar bill from her apron pocket and gave it to me and I thanked her and she told us good-bye and started to close the garage doors.

She stopped, though, and walked over to us. There was a sad look on her face.

"Those magazines, William—do you think they'll help? With the war, I mean."

"They sure will, Mrs. Zielinski," he said. "You'd be surprised how much they'll help."

She smiled and looked like she felt better about it. "Thanks, boys," she said, and Gunner and I watched while she locked the garage and headed for her house.

"See you in the morning, Shadow."

"See you, Gunner."

Chapter Ten

GUNNER CAME OVER FOR SUPPER ONE NIGHT
that week and he came early enough to help me with the
model. I really didn't need all that help on the B-24, but
it was about the only way Billy and I could be together
without Shirley butting in. Mom and Shirley were
working in the kitchen, so I shut my bedroom door so
Billy and I could have some privacy.

The fuselage was finished and we worked on the
wings. Billy sat at my desk and I sat next to him on a

kitchen chair. With a razor blade, he cut the wing struts that are printed on those thin sheets of balsa wood. You have to be real careful when you cut them out or the balsa wood will split, but that didn't give Billy any trouble at all.

In no time he had all the struts done. Then we started putting together one side of the wing, pinning the struts to the plans, and bending the long, thin strips of balsa wood over the struts and pinning them in place. When you get them just so, you squeeze a drop of airplane glue onto the joints. When I do it I get everything all gloppy with glue and make a real mess of it. Not Billy.

"Wish I could make models as good as you do, Billy."

"You can."

"Aw, I can't and you know it."

"I don't mean now, today, Shadow. I mean after you've had more practice. After you've done it a lot more."

"Yeah, but you're so good at everything you do with your hands."

Gunner laughed. "You just have to take your time, Shadow," he said. "Don't rush—you rush, you mess up."

Billy had me do the next stringer alone, and I did it slowly as I could. "A little less glue on the next joint," he said.

We kept at it and when we got to a place where we had to wait for all the glued joints to dry and harden, we just talked. Billy leaned back on the desk chair and I stretched out, belly down, on the lower bunk.

He was frowning. "Whatcha thinking about, Gunner?"

At first he didn't answer. "A buddy," he said finally.

"Guy named Fitz—waist gunner on our crew. He took a hunk of shrapnel over Germany—hit bad, poor Fitz— and we were a long way from home.

" 'Course we couldn't do much to help him—no medical supplies on board, and even if we did have some, nobody knows how to use 'em, so we dumped Fitz."

"Dumped him?"

He turned to me and nodded. "We rigged his chute to open and let him down through the bomb bay doors. We were hours away from home and he was bleeding bad—he couldn't have lasted more than an hour. Maybe less. So we dumped Fitz, hoping somebody would find him and give him the medical help he needed."

Gunner said he guessed we never hear about such things on the home front. "But Shadow, that sort of thing happens plenty over there. At least a guy has a chance that way, even if he does get captured by the Nazis. Keep him aboard and he's a goner, sure."

"Did Fitz ever get back?"

Billy shook his head. "Never heard a word about him. Missing in action over Germany's all we know."

"Gee," I said. It was a dumb thing to say, but I couldn't think of anything else.

"Hey there, Shadow, I'm sorry," he said, brightening up. "Didn't mean to get off on that. No more hairy war stories, I promise."

So I sniffed the air and Billy did, too. He grinned.

"Pork roast," I said.

"And applesauce?" Billy asked.

"Yeah. Mom's been saving up ration points."

Billy said something that sounded like "Mmmmmm,"

and for a long time neither of us said anything and it was good just being with Billy, not having to talk or anything. Just being together. And after a while there was a knock on the door and Mom said it was time to wash up.

We ate in the dining room and even used the good tablecloth and our very best dishes. The real china ones. The meal was real good and Billy seemed to enjoy it as much as I did.

"How's the food where you're stationed, Billy?" asked Dad.

"Not bad," he said, "but it's not good. Nothing like this. A delicious meal, Mrs. Simpson," he said, looking at Mom. She smiled and fluttered her eyelids and looked down at her plate, then thanked him.

"Are those powdered eggs they make you eat as horrible as they say they are?" asked Mom. "Just the other night Bob Hope joked about them."

Billy swallowed what he was chewing, then said powdered eggs *were* pretty awful. "It's funny, though. I've gotten to where I don't mind them too much. What bothers me is the sight of *fresh* eggs—scrambled, sunnyside up, over easy, no matter how they're cooked."

"Why's that, Bill?" asked Shirley. "I'd guess you'd like having fresh eggs."

"You'd think so, wouldn't you? Almost every morning we're served powdered eggs. But on the mornings we have to fly a mission we have *fresh* eggs cooked to order, any way we want them. I guess they want us to have a good meal under our belts so we'll perform better. It's gotten to where fresh eggs for breakfast means another mission, and a lot of us just—well, we can't stand the sight of 'em anymore. If I never see another pair of eggs, sunnyside up, staring at me from my breakfast plate again, it'll suit me just fine."

All of us laughed and Mom and Shirley got up to clear the table for dessert. I hoped it wouldn't be rhubarb.

"Then the missions are bad," said Dad, as the three of us men waited at our places.

"They're bad," said Gunner. "Some are worse than others, but they're all lousy. It's the last ten minutes, as we approach our target, that are the worst, though." Shirley and Mom had come back into the dining room to listen. Mom stood in the doorway and Shirley sat sideways in her chair.

"We're flying in formation, see," Billy went on. "Hundreds of planes—our B-24s and the B-17s, all of us from a bunch of little airfields scattered all over England.

"When the weather's clear and we have good fighter cover, it's not too bad. But sometimes the fighters can't go all the way with us, especially on some of our longer missions, because they don't have the range we have. That means part of the time we're just sitting ducks for those Nazi fighters.

"Each bomber waits to unload on the target at the exact same location the lead bomber unloads.

"Trouble is, for that to be accurate, we have to lock into a real tight formation for the last ten minutes or so—after we reach what they call the 'initial point'—as we approach a target. We can't break formation for anything, unless we're hit bad. We can't take any evasive action or make fancy maneuvers to avoid the fighters or antiaircraft guns, so we're just stuck there. Believe me, those ten minutes seem to last forever."

Mom shivered and went back to the kitchen, but Shirley sat there, looking up at Billy. For a minute it seemed tears came to her eyes, because they glistened, but then she smiled, stood up, and gently touched Billy on the shoulder as she turned and followed Mom into the kitchen.

Dessert wasn't rhubarb. It was lazy daisy cake, and next to devil's food, it's my favorite.

"We have some good news, Billy," Mom said over dessert. "We had a letter today from Russell and he thinks he can get a furlough at Thanksgiving."

"Hey, swell," Gunner said. "Bet you're eager to see him."

"It'll be good," Dad said, leaning back in his chair. "I can't deny that. It's a while since he's been home."

"It'd be nice if someday we could get leave at the same time," said Billy. "I'd sure like to see Russ again."

"Maybe next time around," Dad said. "Imagine you boys will have plenty of catching up to do."

"I know we will," said Billy.

Nobody said anything for a minute or so. I guess everybody was thinking about all Russ and Gunner would have to tell each other.

And then Dad pushed his chair away from the table and looked over at Shirley and Gunner and asked them what they had planned for the rest of the evening.

Gunner said they might take a walk up to the park. "It's such a nice night," Shirley said.

Dad thought that was a good idea and he said he'd like

to walk off some of that dinner himself. "But I'd better be getting to bed," he said. "That alarm clock goes off mighty early."

Gunner looked across at me. "Shadow, you want to go with us?" When he said that, I could tell Shirley kicked Billy under the table.

"No," said Mom, before I could open my mouth to say yes. "I'm afraid Bobby had better stay home and help me with the dishes and then get to bed. You two have a nice walk, but not too late, though."

Gunner and Shirley left. Dad went to bed. Mom washed. I dried. Mom talked to me, but I was so mad I only said "yeah" and "uh-uh" and "huh?" and she got peeved at me for sulking.

And when I dropped one of the good dinner plates —honest, it *was* an accident—and it shattered into a hundred pieces, she sent me off to bed and said she'd finish up herself. She wasn't at all happy. Neither was I.

When I went into the bathroom to wash up and brush my teeth, I snuck into Shirley's bedroom and hid her hair curlers where she'd have plenty of trouble finding them. That night she couldn't put up her hair and the next morning she had to go to school with straight hair and she was furious at me for a week.

I didn't care.

Chapter Eleven

THERE WEREN'T MANY DAYS LEFT OF GUN-
ner's furlough and it seemed every day I saw him less
than the day before. Not Shirley. She saw plenty of him.
Almost every afternoon after school he met her at the
bus stop and they'd walk home holding hands. Evenings
they took walks or listened to records or went to the
show or bowling, even on school nights.

One Friday night he took her to a dance at school, and
Shirley got to wear Mom's new high-heeled shoes. The

heels were higher than the ones on her own Sunday shoes, so for two evenings before the dance, Shirley put them on and practiced walking around the house in them. She sure looked silly, clippety-clopping in rolled-up jeans and high-heeled shoes. She practiced so she wouldn't fall off the shoes at the dance. If that happened she said she'd just *die!* I think it's stupid to wear shoes that you have to *practice* wearing. She was going to wear her new party dress—it's blue and makes a crinkly sound when she moves—and Mom was letting her borrow a pair of her silk stockings.

The second Shirley got home from school the afternoon of the dance, she started getting ready. She used bubble bath and must've sat in the bathtub for an hour. Nobody can get so dirty that you have to soak *that* long, especially not Shirley. She had her hair in curlers and she pressed her dress and at supper she was too excited to eat more than a few bites, even though we had Swedish meatballs.

I had to do the dishes alone because Mom was busy fixing Shirley's hair and helping her dress. You'd think a person who is seventeen years old could comb her own hair and get dressed without her mother's help.

But I have to admit that when she came out to the kitchen to show Dad and me, Shirley looked swell. She smelled good, too, because she had used some of Mom's Evening in Paris perfume.

"You look mighty pretty, baby," Dad said. "Billy's a lucky young fella." Mom had Shirley spin around to make certain her slip wasn't showing.

"I'm so excited—I have a feeling Bill might give me

his gunner's wings tonight," she said, when she was done spinning.

"Why would he do that?" I asked.

She smiled and her teeth looked real white because of all the lipstick she was wearing. "Well, it's sort of like when a boy gives a girl his high school class ring or when a college guy gives his girl friend his fraternity pin."

I emptied the dishpan down the drain and rinsed it.

"Hmmmm—sounds serious," said Dad. "Aren't you a little young to get engaged?"

"Not really engaged, Daddy," she said. "More like engaged to *be* engaged."

"And Billy is such a fine young man," Mom said.

I asked Shirley what she'd do with the wings if he gave them to her.

"Wear them," she said. "Every day I'd wear them, on my blouse or sweater."

All at once I felt sad, or maybe hurt, and I wished Billy would give *me* his gunner's wings instead. Only I wouldn't wear them because they might get lost. I'd put them on my bedroom wall with the Eighth Air Force patch and all the B-24 pictures and everything. They'd be a neat souvenir and I'd appreciate them a whole lot more than she would.

When the doorbell rang we all went to greet Gunner.

He was in his dress uniform and he looked swell. He smelled of shaving lotion, and his crew cut was brushed just so, and his shoes looked like he must've spent all afternoon shining them. When I saw the silver wings on his uniform I wished I had a pair like them. Before I put them up on the wall I'd wear them to school and show all

★ 87 ★

the guys. Nobody in Miss Connelly's room had a pair of gunner's wings.

"You look beautiful, Shirl," he said to her. He didn't even seem to notice Mom and Dad and me.

"So do you," Shirley said, and she got flustered, and laughed. "You look *handsome*, I mean. Boys aren't supposed to look beautiful."

"Here," he said, and he handed her a fancy box tied with a ribbon.

"A gardenia!" Shirley squealed, when she opened the box. She kissed Billy on the cheek—right there in front of all of us—and he had to wipe off the lipstick with his hanky. I wondered what Mrs. Eckert would think of that.

Mom pinned it to Shirley's dress. "Just beautiful," Mom said, "and how good it smells!" Ladies always get gushy about the way flowers smell and look.

"By the way, Pa let me borrow the car tonight," said Billy, taking the car keys from his pocket, "so we won't have to take the bus."

"Now, you two run along," said Mom, "and have yourselves a marvelous evening." Shirley kissed Mom and Dad, but I stepped back before she could even *try* kissing me. I don't think she would have, anyway. Then they were out the door, down the steps, and walking toward the curb, where Mr. Eckert's car was parked. It was chilly outside. Before long we'd be having a frost.

Dad stepped onto the porch. "Don't do anything *I* wouldn't do," he called after them. Mom told him to hush, but she laughed.

I could hear Billy and Shirley laugh, too, and Billy

turned his head back over his shoulder and hollered for Dad not to worry. I went to the sofa at the front windows and knelt on it and watched them. Billy opened the car door for Shirley and she got inside. Then he walked around the car and slid into the seat behind the steering wheel and in a second they drove off.

Mom and Dad went back to the kitchen to have a cup of coffee, but I stayed there, kneeling on the sofa, staring out the window.

It was time for "Henry Aldrich" on the radio, but that's a real funny program and I didn't even feel like laughing that night, so I just kept looking out the front window for a long, long time. I was still watching when Doc turned out the lights and closed the drugstore for the night.

I thought lots about Billy and Shirley—Billy, mostly —and I wondered if he would really give her his gunner's wings.

Chapter Twelve

GUNNER WAS GUEST OF HONOR AND IT WAS
about the best block party I'd ever been to, only I didn't
have any fun. The day of the party I was in trouble with
both Mom and Dad, but for different reasons. Both
reasons were Juicy's fault.

Saturday morning, the day after Billy took Shirley to
the dance, Juicy came over early. We sat on the back
steps and talked.

"Need your help," he told me.

"Doin' what?"

"Politics," he said. It sounded important. Juicy pushed his hair out of his eyes. He has red hair and he's real freckly, so he looks all orange, except for his bright green eyes.

"What do you mean, *politics?*"

"My old man asked me to ring doorbells and give people Roosevelt buttons and ask them to put a poster in their window." He showed me a poster. It had a big picture of President Roosevelt on it.

"But we're Republican," I said.

"That's okay. No one'll know."

"Besides, it's Saturday. I've got my chores."

"You can do your chores after."

"Okay—for a while. Just so Dad doesn't find out. He'd have a fit!"

Juicy crossed his heart and said he hoped he'd die if he ever told my father.

"I've never been a politician—how do you do it?"

"A cinch. You be the lady of the house. Go inside and I'll ring your front doorbell."

"Good morning, ma'am," said Juicy, when I opened the door. "My name is Arnold O'Brien, and I'd like to ask you to vote for President Roosevelt in the election next month."

"I'm sorry, Arnold, but we're all Republicans in this house," I said. "We're going to vote for Mr. Dewey." I slammed the door shut. Juicy rang the bell again.

"No, dummy, you're supposed to say you're a Democrat and you love Roosevelt and plan to vote for him. So then I give you a couple of these buttons and ask you to put a Roosevelt poster in your front window where everybody can see it."

"Then what do I say, Arnold?"

"Quit calling me Arnold."

"You said that's who you were."

"Well, skip it for now. You tell me you'd be tickled to death to have the button and poster, so you stick the pin on your dress and put the poster in your front window."

I pinned the button on my shirt, then put the poster in the center window, not far from the service flag.

"Then I tell you, 'Thank you, lady,' and I go off to the next house. Understand?"

"That's all there is to being a politician?"

"That's all. It's simple."

Juicy gave me some posters and buttons and for an hour we rang doorbells. It's amazing how many Republicans live in our neighborhood. Only two houses had any Democrats living in them. It wasn't hard to tell that Dewey was going to win the election in November. Roosevelt didn't have a chance.

At the end of the third block I told Juicy I couldn't be a politician anymore because I had to get home and scrub the kitchen floor and clean the toilet and stuff. "You going to the show?" I asked.

"Can't," he said. "Promised my old man I'd hand these out."

"Me, neither. Why don't you come over when you're done? Maybe we can do something." He said he would.

When I got home Shirley was up. "It was a wonderful dance," she said, even though I hadn't asked her. "We just had the most marvelous time. Everybody thought

Bill looked so handsome in his uniform. Afterward we had an ice-cream soda at the Buffalo." The Buffalo is a fancy ice-cream parlor up on Irving Park Boulevard.

"Did Billy give you his wings?"

She just shook her head and looked sad. "But there's still time," said Shirley. I was relieved to hear that Billy had at least *some* brains left.

I got right to work and by the time Juicy came over I had finished my chores and was working on the B-24. It was beginning to shape up. The wings and fuselage were done and I had begun to build the split tail. I asked Juicy what he wanted to do.

"Heck, I don't know. Can't play ball—Ralph and Ed went to the show. Besides, it's raining."

We went into my bedroom. There was nothing good on the radio. There never is on Saturday afternoon. So we looked at comic books.

"You feel okay?" Juicy asked after a while.

"Yeah. Why?"

"'Cause you look pale, like you're coming down with something. I hope it ain't catching."

"I feel okay," I said. I looked in the dresser mirror, but it was too dark to tell. I felt my forehead. It didn't feel hot, but I couldn't tell for sure. Then Juicy felt my forehead and he shrugged, like maybe it *was* hot.

There had been a lot of infantile paralysis in Chicago that year. An epidemic. Mom always reads in the paper about how many people are dying of infantile paralysis and then she worries. She always talks about how awful infantile paralysis is and she won't let me swim in the park pools or at Lake Michigan beaches, and she doesn't like me going to the show or anyplace where there's a crowd.

Juicy's mother lets him go anywhere he wants, but she makes him wear a little cloth bag with camphor in it, tied on a string around his neck. You get used to the smell. Before the camphor he had garlic in the bag and that was even worse. His mom is positive the garlic and camphor kill the germs and keep him healthy. I think he stinks so bad everybody stays away from him, so he doesn't get their germs.

Anyway, I went to look in the bathroom mirror. Juicy followed me. I turned on the light and leaned close to the mirror. He was right. I did look pale.

"If Mom thinks I'm sick she won't let me go to Billy's block party tomorrow," I said. "What should I do?"

"Hide from your old lady."

"Dummy—I can't do that. I've got to eat supper with her, and breakfast. How can I hide?"

Juicy shrugged. "You got any good medicine in here?" he asked, and he opened the medicine cabinet above the sink. We both looked.

"What's this?" asked Juicy, and he took a bottle from the bottom shelf. He read the label aloud.

"GABY Leg Makeup," he said. "Hmmmmmm."

That's what Mom and Shirley use because you can't hardly get nylon or even silk stockings on account of the war. They smear makeup on their legs and it looks like they're wearing hosiery. "Shake well before using," Juicy read on, and he shook the bottle. The stuff inside was a light, orangy brown color.

"Says here you're supposed to smooth it on with a

sponge or cotton. Work up from ankle. Allow to dry thoroughly and brush off excess. Will not spot or rub off. This shade suntan." He looked at me, his face brightening.

"Simp, this is exactly what you need!" he said, snapping his fingers. "We'll just smear on this stuff and your old lady'll never know you have infantile paralysis. You'll be able to go to the block party."

"Really?"

"Sure. Take off your clothes."

"But it's just my face that looks pale."

"Yeah, but if you have pale arms and legs and a healthy face, she'll know something's fishy. Besides, the label says to start at your ankles and work up."

I should have known better. Juicy's always getting me into trouble. Shirley was in her bedroom—I could hear the radio—so I closed the bathroom door and peeled down to my undershorts.

"All the way," said Juicy. I sighed and took off the shorts. We found some cotton and both of us got to work. It felt funny. We started on my ankles, like the directions said. It must've taken us ten minutes to get the job done. We almost emptied the bottle.

"How do I look?" I asked.

"Healthy. You could be half-dead and your old lady'd never guess you were sick." I looked in the mirror. I looked healthy, all right. I looked like I had spent all summer on the beach.

Juicy laughed. "You look like that picture of Hiawatha in the library at school," he said. "All's you need now is a feather in your hair."

I dressed and we cleaned up the bathroom. Then Juicy went home and I worked some more on the model. I tried doing it slowly, like Billy said, but it seemed it would take forever that way.

When I heard the back gate slam I knew Mom was home from work, and I didn't want her to see how healthy I was just yet. I'd surprise her at the supper table. I hurried into bed and pretended to be asleep, only I must've really fallen asleep then, because the next thing I knew, Dad was calling me to supper.

Shirley wasn't home. She was eating at the Eckerts' house, and she and Billy were going to the show afterward.

It didn't take Mom more than a second to notice how healthy I looked.

"Bobby!" she shrieked. "What's happened to you?" She leaned toward me for a closer look.

Just then Dad spotted the Roosevelt button pinned to my shirt. I had forgotten all about it. "What is *that* thing doing on your shirt?!"

He yanked it off and flung it across the kitchen toward the trash can. "A Roosevelt pin," I said, in a squeaky voice. "I was helping Juicy be a politician." Dad hardly ever yells at me, but when he does, he means business.

"Just what is that supposed to mean?"

"It means we went from door to door asking people to vote for President Roosevelt in the election next month. And we gave them pins to wear and posters to put in their front windows. Like the one in ours."

"In ours?" He pushed back from the table so hard he almost knocked his chair over. He stomped to the living room and was back in a second.

"Edna, will you look at this," he said to Mom. "And in our front window!" He held up the poster of President Roosevelt for Mom to see, then tore it into little pieces and tossed them into the garbage. Dad doesn't like President Roosevelt.

Then he dug his fork into his plate of supper like he was mad at it. He wasn't finished with me, though. I could tell. He was just thinking up what to holler at me next. Mom beat him to it.

"What *I* want to know, young man, is what you did to your skin!"

"Leg makeup."

"On your face? What on earth for?"

"I didn't want you to think I had infantile paralysis, because then you wouldn't let me go to Billy's block party. Juicy said I looked pale, like I was sick."

"Well, how do you feel?" She put her palm on my forehead. Her hand felt hotter than my forehead.

"I feel okay. I guess I'm just pale."

"Well, you march right into that bathroom and wash it off."

"All of it?" I asked, pushing away from the table.

"Every last bit!"

"But it's all over me—the directions on the label said to start at the ankles."

Leaning back in her chair, she shook her head. "And I suppose you used my new bottle of GABY," she said, and I nodded. "Any left?"

"Not much. When you start at your ankles, you sure use a lot of it."

Mom shook her head again and I asked if she wanted me to go wash it off that second and she said no, for me to finish my supper and then take a good hot bath.

I picked at my food. I didn't feel much like eating anyway, because it was macaroni again, but Mom kept telling me to eat so I choked it down. I didn't want to hear a word about those poor, starving Chinese kids. She worries more about them than she does about me.

"How long was it there?" asked Dad.

"The makeup?"

"*No*, that poster—in our front window!"

"Since about eight o'clock, when Juicy and I started being politicians."

Dad covered his face with his hands and shook his head. "The neighbors," he said softly. "They'll all think I'm voting for Roosevelt!" When he says "Roosevelt" it sounds like a swear word.

Dad lectured me then about what fine men Thomas Dewey and John Bricker are. They're the Republicans running for president and vice-president in November.

"Democrats," he said, shaking a finger at me, "are different. They're not our kind of people."

I swallowed a mouthful of macaroni and washed it down with milk. "But Juicy's a Democrat, and he isn't different. Except he has red hair and he spits when he talks." I wondered if all Democrats spit when they talk and if that's what Dad meant about them being different.

"Never you mind," he said. "Democrats are—well, different. Just take my word for it."

We finished supper in silence. Nothing more was said about me being a politician or smearing myself all over with leg makeup. Later Dad gave me a button. "Wear this one!" he told me. It said, "Win the War Quicker with

Dewey and Bricker." I pinned it to my shirt right away, so Dad could see I had learned my lesson.

It turned out I got to stay up later that night than I thought I would because Mom made me take *three* baths to get off all the leg makeup. It was awful.

One bath a week is bad enough, but three in one night was terrible. I hope I'll never again have to take three baths in one day as long as I live.

If being a Republican means you have to take that many baths, I'd rather be a dirty Democrat. Even if they are different.

Chapter Thirteen

AS SOON AS WE GOT HOME FROM CHURCH THE next day, Mom and Shirley took off their Sunday dresses and put on chenille housecoats and tied aprons over them, and started frying chicken. All the ladies have to take food to the block parties and Mom decided on fried chicken. Everybody talks about how wonderful her fried chicken is, so that's what she always takes.

"I hate to think of Billy leaving on Friday," Shirley said, as she turned a piece of chicken in the pan. "It seems as though he only just got home."

"I know, dear," said Mom. "We all feel that way. But you, especially." With a fork in each hand, Mom lifted pieces of chicken from her pan, let them drip for a second, then put them on a rack to cool.

Dad was at the kitchen table reading the Sunday *Tribune* and I sat across from him, looking at the funnies and half listening to Shirley and Mom. Dick Tracy was still chasing the crook called Shaky, and didn't seem close to catching him.

Mom loaded her pan with more chicken and it sizzled and splattered and then she turned the pieces slowly, over and over. The chicken smelled so good my stomach growled.

"What Bill does is so dangerous," said Shirley. "I'll worry every minute he's gone."

"Of course you will," Mom said, nodding. "I thank God every day our Russell's in Texas."

"I'd give anything if Bill was going to Texas or someplace like that, instead of back to England to fly more of those awful missions," Shirley said.

"Then it's serious with you two?" asked Dad, putting aside the newspaper. Looking down into the frying pan, Shirley nodded and said yes, that it was.

"Aren't you a little young to be that serious?"

"Oh, it's not like we're going to run off and get married before he leaves," she said, looking at Dad. "It's more like we're just going to—well, *wait* for each other."

For a while she and Mom worked at the chicken, then Shirley turned to Mom and said, "I've never been in love before—just crushes on some of the fellas at school. But what I feel toward Bill just has to be love. I know it does.

"We've even talked about things like how many children we'll have and what we'll name them, and—" She sniffed and then sobbed. "Oh, Mom, what if something happens to Bill? I'd die, I'd just die!" And all of a sudden she ran from the kitchen, crying.

"Carl, you take over here," Mom said. "I've got to go to her." She tied her apron on Dad and he stepped to the stove and began turning the pieces of chicken.

A long time later when Mom and Shirley came back to the kitchen, both had real red eyes. They didn't talk any more about Billy then, but I knew they were thinking about him.

I thought about Billy, too, and about how awful I'd feel if anything happened to him. And then I tried to put it out of my mind because I don't like to think about sad things. I had finished reading the funnies, but I read them again to keep from thinking about Billy.

Even though it was still only October and we hadn't had Thanksgiving or even Halloween yet, the McGowans had decorated their basement with twisted streamers of red and green crepe paper, and the long tables the McGowans borrow from their church were covered with white paper and had red and green streamers laid down the middle. Up front, right behind the main table, was a Christmas tree, decorated with ornaments and tinsel. Don't ask me where they got a Christmas tree in October, but this was to be a Christmas party for Billy, because he would be over in England when real Christmas came around. Captain McGowan had asked the neighbors to bring a little gift for Billy, if they wanted to, wrapped like a Christmas present. Lots did. I put our package under the tree with the rest.

★ 102 ★

Billy must have seen us the minute we stepped inside, because he made his way through the crowd and came up to say hello. He had to sit up at the head table, he said, and he asked Shirley if she would sit with him. She looked at Dad, and he smiled and said sure, just so long as she minded her manners and didn't put her elbows on the table or try to eat her peas with her knife. She groaned and said, "Oh, Daddy."

Our platters of chicken went on the big table over by the furnace. It was already loaded with food. Besides the chicken, there was a ham and a big beef roast, and a couple of bowls of meatballs and two kinds of potato salad and Jell-O rings and spaghetti casserole and a heaping plate of Polish kielbasa sausage and homemade breads and cakes and pies and cookies and everything. I hadn't seen so much food since before the war.

After what had happened the day before, I wasn't at all surprised that I couldn't sit with Juicy. Mom and Dad made me sit between them where they could both keep an eye on me. I felt like a little kid.

Most everybody was there. Jeannine sat with some other high school friends and she was acting very snooty, as usual. Juicy was at a table way across the basement and he tossed me a wave when he caught my attention. He was with Ed and Ralph and I'd have given anything to be sitting with them. All of them were wearing Roosevelt buttons. I wished I'd worn my Dewey one.

"Seats, everybody!" shouted Captain McGowan, tapping his spoon on his water glass. "Please take your seats!"

When it was quiet, he led the pledge of allegiance,

and then Mrs. Zielinski played our national anthem and we all joined in singing. Mrs. Ohlson, the Baptist, asked the blessing. I thought she'd never finish. It seemed like she prayed for every single meatball, one at a time, and I was afraid the food would spoil before we could eat it. Finally we did eat, and it was worth waiting for. I went through the line three times and would've gone a fourth if Mom hadn't said no.

When everybody finished eating, the ladies cleared the dishes away and the men took down the tables and leaned them against the wall. Then we all sat on chairs facing the Christmas tree.

Captain McGowan began the program by introducing Billy, and he asked Billy to stand up and everybody clapped. His face got red and he grinned and waved and sat down again, quick as he could. When Billy's parents were introduced, Mrs. Eckert stood and smiled, giving everybody a chance to see that she had been to the beauty parlor on Saturday afternoon. Mr. Eckert popped up and down before anybody knew it and he got redder than Billy.

After that, the captain made a speech about Billy's war record and about how he was a hero. His parents looked real proud of him. Mrs. Eckert wiped at her eyes with a hanky. Billy looked like he wanted to crawl under the table.

The captain was making some announcements then, when all of a sudden, he cocked his head to one side and said, "What's *that* I hear up on the rooftop?"

Just as he said it, Mrs. Zielinski started playing "Santa Claus Is Coming to Town." There was a loud stomping on the stairs and everybody looked over and there was Mr. Geannopoulos, who lives down the block, wearing a dime-store Santa Claus suit and going, "Ho, ho, ho." He doesn't even need any pillows when he plays Santa.

It was hard to understand what he said through the mask and beard, but between the "ho-hos" he asked Billy if he had been a good little boy, and everybody howled and clapped, and Billy got red again and said he had. Then Mr. Geannopoulos sat down on a folding chair next to the Christmas tree and handed Billy the presents, one at a time. Billy's face stayed red the whole time he opened the packages, and he looked as though he wished he was someplace else, like maybe in the tail of a B-24.

He got things like a tube of shaving cream and socks and hankies and three bottles of shaving lotion and a new billfold—that was from us and it had a secret pocket in it—and he got a lot of Christmas cards with dollar bills in them. The Tomaszek sisters gave him a yellow muffler their mother had knit. While Billy opened presents, Mrs. Zielinski played carols.

When the last package had been opened, Gunner stood and said, "Gee, everything is swell and I just don't know what to say, except, thanks, everybody. Thanks a lot." Mrs. Zielinski played "Silent Night," and then, without anybody saying to, all of us joined hands and turned to face Billy and we sang. It seemed funny singing a Christmas carol in October. It sounded nice, though, except that some of the ladies got real sniffly and they couldn't blow their noses because they were holding hands.

When "Silent Night" was over, everybody stood there wondering what would happen next, when all of a sudden Mrs. Zielinski started playing "The Beer Barrel Polka." That really zipped things up.

Captain McGowan cupped his hands around his mouth and called out, "First dance, our guest of honor and his lovely young lady friend, Shirley Simpson!" Chairs were pushed against the walls and the captain sprinkled dance wax all over the concrete floor. Then he told Shirley and Billy to have a go at it. Shirley looked scared to death. They danced on the slippery floor and all the neighbors stood around in a big circle, smiling, calling to them, clapping hands in time with the polka music. Soon a few other people were dancing.

Just then I saw Juicy take a running start and he slid clear across the floor on the dance wax. It was a good slide, even better than you usually get on real ice. I saw that Mom and Dad were over by the washing machine talking with some new neighbors. If Juicy could do a good slide on the dance wax, I could do a better one!

I made a quick, short run and took off. It was a swell slide except that I hit a greasy spot where somebody had dropped a slice of ham earlier, and I went flying and landed smack on my rear end.

My teeth banged together like a mousetrap and I saw stars. Tears came to my eyes but I made myself not cry. Juicy and the guys laughed like it was the funniest thing they ever saw. If I'd been closer I'd have poked them all in the nose. Everybody stopped dancing and looked at me and Dad was frowning. I was on my feet in a second and off toward the far end of the basement. My bottom hurt worse than a spanking would have and I could hardly walk.

Gunner came over and asked if I was okay and I told him sure and he nodded and punched me soft on my arm, then went back to Shirley. I turned away because I didn't want him to see the tears in my eyes.

By then the floor was filled with dancers. Even Mom and Dad danced. All the ladies wanted to dance with Billy, so they kept cutting in on Shirley. She danced plenty with Billy, though, and with some of the husbands on our block. One of the old Tomaszek sisters went up to tell Billy good-bye because they had to get home and look after their mother, and Billy grabbed her and gave her a few spins around the floor. She about fainted.

Us guys were drinking soda pop and a lot of the grown-ups were drinking beer. Captain McGowan had filled a big laundry tub with ice and quart bottles of beer from Vito's tavern. Somebody had a bottle of something stronger, and a lot of the men went behind the furnace where their wives couldn't see them, to have a drink of it.

When Mrs. Zielinski took a rest, the captain played records on his phonograph. They were just the usual love and dance songs. One of the records was Bing Crosby singing "White Christmas," and Billy and Shirley danced real slow to that one, looking right into each other's eyes.

For a while I got to be with Juicy and the other guys, but I had to be careful of what I did, because I knew I'd better not let Mom or Dad catch me so much as looking cross-eyed or I'd really be in a mess. Then the guys went off to fool around behind the furnace. Ralph said they were going to sneak some beer, but I knew they wouldn't really. I could almost feel Mom's eyes watching me, so I just sat and watched the dancing. Believe me, it was about as exciting as watching paint dry.

Everybody seemed to be having fun but me. I would like to have talked with Gunner for a while, but he was too busy dancing and having fun.

The basement was hot and smelled of sweat. Mrs. Abford got sick and threw up by the washing machine and her husband had to take her home. A lot of the crepe-paper streamers had come down and there were torn pieces of them on the floor, and once Mr. Bunesco slipped while he was dancing with Mrs. McConville and they fell into the Christmas tree and knocked it over, but nobody got hurt. They broke a bunch of ornaments, though.

It was a pretty good block party, but just sitting, watching, isn't much fun, so I didn't care at all when Dad said it was time for us to go home. He let Shirley stay later and Billy would walk her home.

While I was undressing I happened to notice the B-24 model on Russ's drawing board, and I wondered if I'd ever get it done. I was in a hard place and I needed Gunner's help. He said he'd come over and give me a hand, but didn't. I was beginning to feel strange about Billy. I still liked him, I guess, but it didn't seem the way it was before. Maybe he didn't like me anymore, now that he was in love with Shirley.

Before I fell asleep I thought about what it would be like having Juicy as my first-best friend, instead of

Gunner. It was fun being with Juicy, even if he spit when he talked, and even if he did get me in trouble all the time and even if he was a Democrat and was different.

Besides, I'll bet Shirley would never even think of falling in love with Juicy.

Chapter Fourteen

TOWARD THE END OF BILLY'S FURLOUGH I
hardly saw him at all, and when I did see him, he wasn't
much fun to be with. Shirley got to see him plenty,
though, and she sure acted like he was fun to be with.

I'd have bet a hundred dollars Gunner would take me
downtown one Saturday to the show at the Oriental or
Chicago Theater, where you get to see a movie *and* a
stage show for one price. But he didn't. Once, a long time
ago, he took me down to the Oriental and we had a swell

★ 110 ★

time. I forget what the picture was, but Blackstone the Magician was the stage show, and he did absolutely amazing things. That's when I decided I wanted to be a magician when I grow up. All I had to do was learn some tricks and buy a tuxedo suit.

Or I thought Billy might have taken me down to the Field Museum, where they have the Egyptian mummies, like you see in the horror movies, and all those swell Indian things. But he didn't. He didn't even take me to the aquarium or the planetarium. He didn't ask me to do *any*thing with him because he was too busy doing everything with Shirley.

As the Saturday when Billy was going to leave got closer, Shirley began acting awful peculiar. One minute she'd be happy and singing and laughing and floating around like she was on a cloud, and the next her eyes would be full of tears and she'd be running off to her bedroom to cry. Don't ask me to explain why. In a million years, I could never explain Shirley.

One afternoon when I was coming home from school, Billy was outside his house, putting up storm windows. Winter would be here before we knew it, he said. He'd washed them all and he was starting to hang and latch them, so I carried the windows out to him from the backyard and handed them up to him on the ladder.

When he got the last one hung, we carried the ladder to the garage and then I went inside the house with him, from window to window, while he hooked the storm windows. I stopped and visited with Mrs. Eckert. She was sitting by the front window, crocheting. Every time I see her inside her house, that's what's she's doing.

Mrs. Eckert had crocheted their dining-room table-cloth and the bedspread in their bedroom, and she had crocheted the doilies on the backs and arms of the sofa and all the easy chairs in their living room. There was a doily she had crocheted on top of the radio and one on each table. There were doilies everywhere you looked in their house. Mr. Eckert always joked that if he didn't keep moving, Naomi would crochet a doily and put it on him, too.

"That was sure a swell block party for Billy," I said to her.

"Just lovely," she said. "All that marvelous food—my, what a spread it was. And those nice gifts. We were terribly proud of our William." She looked at me while she talked, but her fingers kept on crocheting. I couldn't imagine how she could crochet without even looking.

Billy had gone into the bathroom to wash up and he came out looking all scrubbed, and he smelled of Palm-olive soap and Pepsodent toothpaste and Old Spice shaving lotion, all at once. His crew cut was brushed, too.

"C'mon, Shadow," he said. "Let's have a root beer —I'm buying."

Doc brought our drinks and when Billy tried to pay him, he waved a hand and said they were on the house. I don't see how Doc makes any money, because he's always giving away root beers and Cokes. Doc stood behind the fountain and talked with us for a while, then went to the back to wait on a lady who needed a kidney plaster.

"How's the plane coming?" Gunner asked.

"It's not. I'm really stuck right now and you told me you'd try to get over and help me."

"Golly, Shadow, I'd forgotten, but don't give up on me. So many things I want to get done before I leave Saturday, and time's running short. I'd like to spend as much time with Ma and Pa as I can."

Yeah, and with Shirley, I thought, but I didn't say it.

"That's okay, Gunner—I understand. Maybe I can get that hard part figured out myself."

Just then the door opened and Shirley came in, a load of books in her arms. Billy saw her reflection in the mirror and swung around, hopped down, and went to greet her. He kissed her and I turned away.

"How's about an ice-cream soda?" he asked.

"I've got to do homework if we're going out tonight," she said, brushing back her hair. "But okay—I'll make time."

Billy and Shirley sat in the rear booth, and I could see them in the big mirror behind the soda fountain. They whispered about something and Shirley shook her head, but Billy said, "C'mon over, Shadow, and have a soda with us."

I shook *my* head. Just then I was so angry, I couldn't say a word. The back cash register jangled and Doc came up front and Billy ordered a pineapple soda for Shirley and an extra thick chocolate malted for himself. Doc came back to the fountain to make the soda and malted, and I sure didn't feel like talking to him then, so I jumped down from the stool and raced out the door without even saying so long or thank you. If Gunner had wanted to have a drink with me, why didn't he stay with me instead of going over to sit with Shirley?

For a second I stood on the sidewalk just outside the door of the drugstore. I was shaking all over and I made fists with both hands, but that didn't help. That's when I decided I hated Shirley and knew for sure that Gunner and I could never be best friends again. It was all changed. Billy and Shirley were in love and he didn't care one bit about me anymore.

Billy came through Doc's doorway on the run and almost knocked me over. He was mad, too.

"Shadow," he said, trying to sound nice, "you come back in here and have a soda with us!"

"I don't want your soda!" I hollered at him. "You can keep it!"

"Listen to me," he said, putting a hand on my shoulder. I jerked away from Billy. There was a break in traffic on Central Avenue and before he could reach out and grab me again, I ran across the street.

"Go back and drink your old malted with *her*," I yelled, but I don't think he heard me because a truck passed by then.

"Shadow!" he called from across the street. "Shadow!" I wanted to go back then and make up with Gunner, but I didn't.

Now I wish I had. I wish I'd told him I was sorry. Instead I ran home and went into my bedroom and shut the door. I didn't ever want to leave the bedroom again.

I never felt more miserable in my life. And it didn't go away.

All that week I had trouble thinking of anything but Billy. Once, in school, I was thinking about how mean I had been to Gunner when all of a sudden I heard my name called out.

"Robert," said Miss Connelly. "Robert Simpson!"

"Yes'm," I said.

"Robert, I asked you a question. Will you please stand and tell me the answer!"

I stood, but I didn't know the answer. I didn't even know the question! I said I didn't know and all the kids laughed, even Juicy, and that night I had to write a composition about why I should pay attention in class. At least she didn't send a note home.

Every night that week Shirley went out with Billy. I stayed home every night. And usually when Billy called for Shirley, I didn't even go out into the living room to say hello. I didn't want to see him.

One afternoon after school, they went to the record shop and he bought her the record, "He Wears a Pair of Silver Wings," which is a real gushy love song about a guy in the air corps. Kay Kayser's band plays it. Shirley almost wore out the record that first week, playing it over and over. "It's *our* song," I heard her tell Mom. Whenever she sang it she got that dreamy look on her face, and it was enough to make me sick.

When I came home from school on Thursday, Billy was out in front of his house, raking leaves . He had a big pile of them. I looked up at the trees and the branches were almost bare. Those leaves he was raking probably were the last ones of the fall. I kept right on walking.

"Hey, Shadow," he called after me. "How's about a root beer?" I shook my head and kept going.

"Wait up, buddy." I could hear his footsteps in the dry leaves. I stopped, but didn't turn around.

"Well, if you won't let me buy you a root beer, at least sit with me on the steps. We need to talk."

"Okay," I said quietly. We sat on our front steps. Billy still held the rake.

"Your nose out of joint, Shadow?"

"What do you think?"

"I think it is—ever since that afternoon in the drugstore. You're sore at me, Shadow, aren't you? Because of me and Shirley—the way we feel about each other."

I shoved my hands into my pockets. There was a tiny hole in my right pocket and my fingertip touched the skin of my leg.

"I don't know, Gunner. Maybe I'm not *really* mad at you. I don't think I could be."

"Then your feelings are hurt?"

I didn't answer right away. I was thinking about what Billy had asked me.

"I guess it is my feelings," I said finally. "We used to be such good friends, you and me. Gosh, Gunner, for a long time we were. And then all of a sudden you don't have time for me because you and Shirley are always together. And Gunner, you act different."

Billy laughed, but not a happy laugh.

"We're still good buddies, Shadow, you and me. The best. We're just the same as we always were, but I like Shirley, too, only in a different way." Rolling the rake handle between his palms, he asked, "Know what I mean?"

I said I did, but I didn't. Not exactly. I just wished I could be with Gunner as much as I used to, back before he went into the air corps. Back when we went to Saturday matinees together at the Times.

"Look, Shadow, you and I are buddies. We always were, we always will be. But Shirley? Well, Shadow, I'm in *love* with Shirley. You've got a great sister, and when I get back, I want to marry her."

Marry? I tried to imagine what it would be like with Shirley married to Gunner. That would make him my brother-in-law. I wondered if we were brothers-in-law, if we would have to fight and argue all the time, the way Russ and I do when he's home. I hoped not.

"Shadow," he said, after a while, "I wish there was something I could say so you'd understand what I'm trying to tell you." And then he snapped his fingers.

"Wait here a sec," he said, jumping up. "Be right back." He trotted over to his house and went in the front door. While he was gone I thought about what he had been saying and I tried to understand it, but didn't have much luck. If he liked me, but *loved* Shirley, wouldn't that mean he thought more of her than he did of me? Before I could figure out the answer to that, Gunner was back. He sat beside me on the step and turned toward me.

"Here, Shadow. I want you to have these."

He opened my coat and tugged at my plaid flannel shirt. I looked down and saw that he was pinning his gunner's wings to it—right above the Dewey button. For an instant, as I turned for a better look, the late afternoon sun caught on the shiny silver wings, almost like a mirror. I felt a shiver go up my back.

"You look swell with those wings on, Shadow," and he touched his fingertips to his forehead, almost like a salute.

"Thanks," I said. "Thanks a lot, Gunner." He smiled and patted me on the shoulder and I sort of saluted back.

"Shirley said you were going to give *her* your wings, and she said that would mean you were engaged."

"Never mind that, Shadow. Shirl knows how I feel,

even without having my wings. And one of these days before long, I'll be buying her an engagement ring."

"What does it mean, Billy—you giving *me* the wings?"

"That we're close buddies, of course. Best friends. Will you buy that?"

"And how," I said. "Shake?"

"Shake." And we did.

"You know, Shadow," Billy said, looking serious, "you're not going to be a kid much longer. One of these mornings you're going to wake up and you'll be a man, and you'll understand what I've been saying. It'll all make sense, about the way it is between you and me and the way it is between Shirley and me. Know what I mean?"

"Yeah, Gunner—I guess I do."

"Swell," he said. "Then let's go get that root beer. My throat's so dry, I'll bet I could drink six of 'em!

"C'mon, double time to the corner."

Chapter Fifteen

SATURDAY MORNING WAS COLD. THERE HAD been a frost—the first that fall—and the sky was full of dark clouds and it looked as though it might rain. Maybe even snow.

I was up early, even before Mom left for work, and I got dressed right away. After breakfast I went to the front window to watch for Gunner. His uncle was going to pick him up about eight-thirty to take him to the train station.

"Do you see him yet?" Shirley called from the bathroom.

"No," I hollered back. "He still hasn't come out of the house."

Just then, the Eckerts' front door opened and Billy stepped onto the porch with his cloth suitcase and duffel bag. He went back inside then and let the storm door close, and I could see him through the glass, hugging and kissing his mother.

"He's coming out now," I called to Shirley. "Gunner's coming out." In a minute she came into the living room, pulling on her navy pea coat. That autumn every high school girl in Chicago must have had a navy pea coat. Under it Shirley had on one of Russ's shirts, her rolled-up blue jeans and saddle shoes with bobby sox.

We watched from inside while Billy kissed his mother again, then turned and closed the door behind him. He pulled his hanky from his pocket and wiped at his eyes.

I opened our front door and Shirley went outside and I followed her. She ran across the lawn, her arms out, and Billy met her and drew her to him. Then he saw me.

"Mornin', Shadow. Kind of chilly."

"Darn chilly," I agreed. I could see my breath. There was still frost on the grass and it crunched under my gym shoes as I walked across it.

The three of us stood talking for a few minutes. Mostly we talked about how cold it was and what time did Billy's train leave and did he think it would be crowded. Dumb things. I couldn't think of anything to say that didn't sound dumb.

Captain McGowan came marching toward us on his

way to work in ladies' shoes at Marshall Field's. Folded under his left arm were the American and service flags. He stopped to talk.

"Leaving now, are you?" he asked Billy.

"Yes, sir—any minute."

The captain looked into Billy's face. "I wish you well, son," he said. "We're all proud of you and what you're doing. Mighty proud." His eyes filled with tears and he looked as though he might cry, but he caught hold of himself. Captain McGowan shook Billy's hand, smiled and nodded to Shirley and me, and marched off. At the Victory Corner he stopped and fastened the American flag to the rope lanyard, hoisted it a few feet, fastened the service flag below it, and then ran the flags to the top of the pole. He secured the rope, then stepped back, looked up at the flag, and saluted. Billy stood at attention and he saluted, too. Captain McGowan turned and marched off toward the Addison Street bus stop.

Gunner held Shirley close to him and they talked quietly and I moved away so I wouldn't hear. I saw Mrs. Eckert watching through the lace curtains in the window, her face right beside the service flag. We waved to each other.

A black Hudson turned off Central Avenue onto our street and made a zigzag turn so that it faced Central again, and pulled up in front of Billy's house.

"He's here," Billy said, even though we all could see. Billy's Uncle George got out of the car and walked over and shook hands with Billy. Mrs. Eckert opened the front door.

"Coffee, George?" she called.

"'Fraid not, Naomi," he said, looking at his watch. "Rush hour traffic's bound to be heavy, and that train won't wait for Billy." Mrs. Eckert stepped back inside and Uncle George asked Billy if he was all set and Billy said he was.

Shirley began to cry. Billy put his arms around her and held her. I went up to the front steps and picked up the duffel bag and Uncle George got the suitcase. We put them in the backseat.

Arms around each other, Billy and Shirley walked slowly toward the car. Already Uncle George was behind the steering wheel.

"Take care, Shadow," said Billy, turning to me. "And remember what I told you." I tried to smile, but it didn't work. I nodded.

"Sure, Gunner, I'll remember."

"And keep an eye on this sister of yours," he said, drawing Shirley closer to him. "And see to it she behaves."

Billy and Shirley looked at each other. He turned to me then and put out his hand and we shook. His hand was icy. Looking up to the front window, he waved to his mother one more time and threw her a kiss.

Then he took my sister in his arms and held her and kissed her. Billy broke away from Shirley, and opened the car door and got in, slamming the door behind him. Rolling down the window, he reached out and Shirley took his hand and held it. Uncle George started the engine and shifted gears.

"You'll write?" Billy asked her.

"Every day." Her cheeks were wet.

Slowly the car moved from the curb and Shirley walked beside it for a few steps before she let go of Billy's hand.

"Love you," he called softly to her.

"Always . . ." she answered.

Shirley came over and put her arm around me and squeezed. Both of us bawled. I didn't care who saw me.

When the Hudson pulled up to the stop sign at Central Avenue, Billy leaned out the open window and grinned. He threw a kiss to Shirley and she blew one back to him. I raised my hand and waved.

"Good-bye, Gunner," I called, but I knew he couldn't hear me. I reached inside my coat and my fingers closed around the wings he had given me.

As the car pulled away into the traffic on Central Avenue, Billy was still waving, but then a trolley bus came along between us and the black Hudson was gone.

Chapter Sixteen

THEN IT WAS NOVEMBER. RUSS CAME HOME ON furlough and stayed until after Thanksgiving. It was swell having him home. It would've been even better if Billy had been there, too.

Gunner was back in England, though, flying those missions in the greenhouse of a B-24, trying to blast Hitler and Goering and all the other Nazis right off the map.

Shirley wrote to Billy every day, just as she had promised, and he wrote her as often as he could. Every day after school she hurried home to see if there was a letter from him. When there was, she would go into her bedroom and close the door and turn on the radio and read it. She never let us read his letters, but she passed along news from Billy and told us how he was getting along.

The same day Billy left, Shirley had taken the Central bus to Irving Park Road and transferred to the streetcar and gone up to the Sears & Roebuck store and bought some olive drab yarn to knit a sweater for Billy. Mom showed her how and helped her get started, but it didn't go very fast. Shirley wanted to get it finished for Christmas, but everybody knew she wouldn't. Dad sometimes teased her by asking, "*What* Christmas?" But she kept working on it, and harder than she'd ever worked on anything before.

I kept busy, too. There was everything I had to do for the war effort, and after school there were usually softball games with Juicy and the guys. On Saturdays I had my chores and on Sundays I usually had to go to Sunday school and church. I wrote a few letters to Russ and Billy, and sometimes I went to the drugstore to talk with Doc and maybe have a root beer. Even though Juicy and I were together a lot, I stayed out of trouble most of the time.

Whenever I could I washed windows and made deliveries for Doc and ran errands and did jobs for neighbors. The money I earned piled up. When Russ was home I told him about the flight jacket I was saving up for and he gave me five dollars toward it. That was more than I needed.

On the day after Thanksgiving I rode the streetcar up

to the army-navy store. The jacket didn't fit. Even the smallest size was too big.

I bought it, anyway. More than I'd ever wanted anything, I wanted to have a flight jacket like Billy's. If it was too big, so what! I'd just grow into it! Besides, I stuffed tissue paper up in the shoulders and when I looked in the mirror and stood with my arms just so, it looked like the jacket fit perfectly. Well, almost.

Some of the guys at school laughed, but I didn't care. They were just jealous because they didn't have one like it. At least I didn't have to wear that old hand-me-down mackinaw that had belonged to Russell.

Sometimes when I was home alone I'd put on the new jacket and pin the wings to it and imagine that I was tail gunner in a B-24 on a bombing raid over Germany. As fast as those Jerry fighters came at me, I'd blast 'em right out of the sky. It seemed so real sometimes that I'd almost swear it was all happening.

A few times I tried to work on the B-24 model, but I was still stuck in that same place. Billy hadn't gotten over to help me again before he left, and I didn't have time just then to work on it myself. So one afternoon when Mom told me to straighten my room, I just put the box and all the loose pieces on the drawing board and lifted the whole thing onto the high shelf in my closet. I'd get back to it after Christmas, when there would be more time.

The election was over. President Roosevelt was elected for a fourth term and Dad stayed mad for almost a whole week afterward. I think he blamed me that Roosevelt won.

The weather was getting colder. In school the little

kids were making Christmas-tree ornaments and drawing snow pictures, and for music class, they were singing carols. Before long Christmas vacation would be here. I was hoping for a Gilbert chemistry set, but I didn't think I'd get one because they were so expensive. Some even came with a microscope. Every time you turned on the radio you'd hear Bing Crosby singing "White Christmas," and I really got tired of that song. Whenever Shirley heard it, she cried. She cried every time she heard "He Wears a Pair of Silver Wings," too. Almost everything made her cry.

At supper every evening Dad talked about the war and told us how it was going. Things were looking pretty good for our forces in both the Pacific and Europe, he had been saying. Our troops were making good advances on all fronts. And then, suddenly, in the middle of December, something called the Battle of the Bulge happened.

Dad said Hitler ordered a lot of his soldiers to make a sudden attack on the Allied forces that had been sweeping through Europe toward Germany. It took the Allies by surprise and the German mechanized units overran a bunch of Allied troops and there were lots of U.S. casualties.

Coming as it did, just before Christmas, it made just about everybody in America feel awful. It was a big setback in the war, and now it looked as though the war was going to go on a whole lot longer than everybody had thought. Maybe it would even last long enough for me to get into the air corps, or something. I wondered what it would be like, fighting in a war. I wondered if I'd be afraid.

And then Glenn Miller, who was just about everybody's favorite bandleader, was missing on an airplane flight between England and Paris. Shirley cried a lot about that, too, but Dad told her maybe the plane would be found and Glenn Miller would be all right. That didn't help Shirley, though. She cried whenever she'd hear the old Glenn Miller songs.

So as Christmas got nearer, spirits got lower. Mom went ahead with baking her holiday cookies and fruit cake, though, and all of us made our Christmas plans and did our Christmas shopping anyway, because Dad said it wouldn't help the war effort one bit if all of us on the home front moped around and let our morale get real low.

One evening the four of us went out and bought a Christmas tree, and on the Saturday night before Christmas, which was December 23, Dad got the decoration boxes out of our storeroom in the basement, and I helped carry them upstairs and we trimmed the tree.

When it was done we turned on the colored lights and sat around the living room looking at the tree and saying how beautiful it was and how nice it was to have the smell of pine in the house, and we were drinking hot chocolate and talking about Christmas and listening to carols on the phonograph.

And then the telephone rang.

Dad answered it. In less than a minute he was back. His face was white and his eyes were wide, like they were looking at something but not seeing it. He was trembling and his mouth was open and he kept shaking his head. He tried to talk, but he had trouble finding his voice.

"The Eckerts—" Dad said finally, almost in a whisper. "They got a telegram. Billy's been . . . *killed in action!*"

Chapter Seventeen

THE MEMORIAL SERVICE FOR BILLY WAS HELD
at the Victory Corner on a cold Sunday afternoon near
the end of January.

I went with Mom and Dad and Shirley, and we stood
near the honor roll, just behind the dining-room chairs
Mr. Gunderson had brought out of his house for Mr. and
Mrs. Eckert to sit on.

Before the service started I looked around and saw
that just about all the neighbors were there, even the old
Tomaszek sisters and old Mrs. Koontz, whose husband

was still in the Veterans Hospital. Doc Delson had locked up his drugstore, put the "Closed" sign in the front door, and come across Central Avenue for the service.

The wind was icy and everybody was bundled up and huddled together to keep warm. The sky was dark gray, and on our way home from church it had begun to snow. Not the big, soft, wet flakes that look pretty when they're falling. It wasn't that kind of snow. It was powdery and dry and fine and the wind blew it every which way in the air, and when it touched the ground it swirled, like little whirlpools, instead of staying put and building up so you can go bellywhopping or make snowballs.

For a while before the service, Mrs. Zielinski played hymns on her accordion, so softly that at times the wind seemed to swallow the sound of the music. She wore a heavy coat and galoshes and a babushka, but no gloves. I know her fingers must have been frozen stiff, but you couldn't tell from her music. I don't think she made a single mistake.

The American flag was at half-staff, as it had been since the day after the Eckerts got that telegram from the government almost a month before. The wind was blowing so hard the afternoon of the memorial service that I was afraid it would rip the flags, but it didn't. The service flag had three gold stars on it now. The new gold star, the one for Billy, was brighter than the old ones for Myron and Stanley.

That night just before Christmas when Dad had told us the Eckerts got the telegram about Gunner being dead, I hadn't believed it. I still don't believe he's dead. Not Billy. I remember all the things we did together and sometimes when I shut my eyes tight I can see his grin, exactly the way it was, and hear the sound of his laugh and of his voice, the way he said "Shadow," and it just doesn't seem possible that he's gone. At first I thought maybe somebody had made a terrible mistake, and that Billy really was all right.

But then Mr. and Mrs. Eckert got a letter from an officer who had been flying the B-24 right behind Billy's plane. He had seen everything. It was after Billy's plane had locked in and was nearing the target, that it was hit by antiaircraft fire, the officer wrote. Even though Billy's pilot had had trouble holding it steady, the ship remained in formation and dropped its load of bombs right on target. By then the plane was flaming, the officer wrote, and as it was making the turn to head back home, it had exploded and gone down. There were no parachutes.

For a while I wondered about what Billy had been thinking those last few minutes of his life, and I wondered what it had been like for him and if he'd been afraid. But then I stopped wondering those things, I stopped trying to imagine what it had been like and if he had been scared, because I didn't want to know.

I wanted to remember Billy laughing and having fun, like the night he and I picked up all those marbles and bubblegum cards that I had dropped, and the afternoon we got poor old Mr. Koontz up onto the Gundersons' roof to "play" the bugle.

As terrible as I felt about Billy, I knew it was even worse for Shirley. At first she didn't even cry. Not a tear. She went around with a strange, faraway look in her eyes, not talking to anybody. She wouldn't eat or do anything and Mom and Dad worried about her. Over and over she played that Kay Kayser record, "He Wears a Pair of Silver Wings." Once I even heard it in the middle of the night when I had to get up to go to the bathroom. And she kept knitting away on that olive drab sweater, like she was determined to finish it.

Shirley's tears came on Christmas morning. All of us were in the living room, sitting around the Christmas tree opening presents. Dad handed her the package Billy had sent her from England. Her fingers shook as she untied the ribbon and removed the paper. It was a linen blouse and she held it to her and squeezed her eyes tight and broke down and started wailing, and Mom went into Shirley's bedroom with her and stayed for a long time. After that she seemed better, but sometimes I'd see her rereading those letters Billy had written to her and there would be tears in her eyes.

Mrs. Zielinski was still playing hymns when the Eckerts came out of their house and walked toward the Victory Corner. Their preacher was with them and Billy's mother walked between him and Mr. Eckert, holding an arm of each. She wore a heavy black coat and had a black scarf tied over her head to keep out the wind and cold. As they came closer, people stepped aside to let them pass, and in a minute the Eckerts were seated in the chairs. Mom leaned over and said something quietly to both of them, and placed a hand on Mrs. Eckert's shoulder, and Mrs. Eckert reached up and patted Mom's hand. Then Shirley leaned forward and hugged Billy's mother and let her hand rest on Mrs. Eckert's shoulder.

Captain McGowan and the preacher whispered about

something, and then the captain nodded to Mrs. Zielin-ski. At the end of that verse of "Rock of Ages," she stopped playing and jammed her frozen fingers into her pockets. Captain McGowan walked up next to the honor roll and began to speak. In the cold air his voice sounded strangely loud.

He talked about Billy and how each of us would remember him in a different way. Neighbor, friend, loved one. He spoke about Billy's service record and what a fine thing—heroic, the captain called it—he had done by going back into action again, even though he hadn't been ordered to.

Twice Captain McGowan had to stop to blow his nose. You could hear people sniffling everywhere. Even Doc Delson. He stood near the edge of the crowd, his bald head bowed, his old gray fedora clutched over his heart.

I glanced at Shirley and saw that her eyes were gazing off into the distance, and tears were streaming down her cheeks. And all of a sudden I knew there was something I had to do. Something important. I knew then, too, that I didn't hate Shirley and I began to understand how it had been between her and Billy. That's what he'd been telling me, only I was too stupid for it to sink in. What a dummy I'd been. And the wings. When he gave me the wings it was like he was giving some whiny little kid a toy. He had really wanted Shirley to have them.

Taking off a mitten, I unpinned Billy's wings from my leather flight jacket. Then I took off my other mitten and reached over and pinned the wings on Shirley's coat. They were lopsided, but there wasn't time to straighten them.

"Bill said you should have them," I whispered, and

then I kissed her cheek and I could taste her tears on my lips. I slipped off then, making my way through the crowd.

"Bobby—come back!" Dad called in a sharp whisper. I didn't go back. I kept going. I had to hurry because there wasn't much time left. Already Captain McGowan was beginning to read aloud the letter the Eckerts got from that officer about how Billy's plane went down. In a few minutes the minister would be speaking.

It didn't take me a half-minute to run home. I let myself in the back door and went straight to the bedroom closet and got Russ's bugle from behind the cigar boxes of bubblegum cards and marbles. Mr. Koontz was still in the hospital and somebody had to play taps for Billy.

As I passed the dresser I glanced at myself in the mirror, and sad as I felt, I almost laughed aloud. I hadn't noticed it before, but I really looked stupid in that flight jacket. Even with the tissue paper in the shoulders, it was almost big enough for two of me. I unzipped it and pulled it off and dropped it on the floor of the closet, then yanked Russell's old mackinaw off its hanger. I put it on and was on my way. I sure didn't need a flight jacket to make me think I was grown up. Maybe next winter it would fit me better. Until then, the mackinaw would be okay.

I ran back through the alley to the Gundersons' backyard. Their ladder was under the back porch, where it had been that day the honor roll was dedicated. I managed to pull it out alone, but getting it propped up against the house was harder than I thought it would be. Once it started slipping sideways and I was sure it would crash to the ground, but I caught it just in time. When it was steady, I climbed to the roof.

It was even colder up there because there was nothing to break the blast of the wind, and the tiny, dry snowflakes swirled all around me. All the trees were bare of leaves now, and over the rooftops I could see the American flag flying way off in Portage Park. It seemed different up there on the roof now, alone, without Mr. Koontz, without Billy. It was bleak and cold and I was shivering and my teeth were chattering like anything and I couldn't stop shaking. Still, I was glad I had on Russ's mackinaw, even though the flight jacket might have been warmer.

Quietly as I could, I inched up the roof to the peak and looked down at the Victory Corner and at Mr. and Mrs. Eckert and at Mom and Dad and Shirley and all the neighbors. Except for the sound of the preacher's voice, everything seemed still. Even the traffic on Central Avenue was quiet.

The minister had finished talking and now he was saying a prayer. Juicy blew his nose real loud as the preacher said, "Amen," and Mrs. Zielinski began to play "The Star-Spangled Banner." I was shivering even more then and the bugle was icy in my hand. I put the other hand over the mouthpiece to warm it, so it wouldn't freeze to my lips. When the last notes of the national anthem faded away, the minister led everybody in saying the Lord's Prayer.

I raised up on my haunches, and when the prayer was about done I stood up, right where Mr. Koontz had stood on that afternoon so long ago. My knees shook like they were made of rubber. The prayer ended and people began to move. The service was done. The minister stepped up to Mrs. Eckert and took her hand. Now!

I lifted the bugle to my lips, took a deep breath, and blew. I didn't rush it. I held all the notes I was supposed to, and I could almost feel the sound leave the horn and drift out over the rooftops in the icy air, maybe even all the way up to Portage Park.

And when I was done blowing taps for my pal Gunner, I stood for a second with tears rolling down my cheeks and with my eyes squeezed tight, remembering.

If only there was some way I could tell him I was sorry about the way I had acted. And there were other things I wished I could tell him, too. But I think maybe Gunner knew and understood.

I brushed at the tears then, and, chewing my lip to keep from crying, climbed down the ladder. I wanted to hurry home and lift the drawing board off the closet shelf and get to work on the B-24. I was sure I'd be able to figure out the problem where I was stuck. I was anxious to get the model finished so I could hang it from the ceiling, but I knew I'd take my time and work slowly and carefully. The way Gunner always had.